ANOTHER TIME

Time Travel Stories

Other Titles from Space Cowboy Books

Complete Poems 1965–2020 – Michael Butterworth

Simultaneous Times Vol. 3 – Various Authors

Simultaneous Times Vol. 2.5 – Various Authors

Simultaneous Times Vol. 2 – Various Authors

Simultaneous Times Vol. 1 – Various Authors

Garbage In, Gospel Out – Jean-Paul L. Garnier

Betelgeuse Dimming – Jean-Paul L. Garnier

Future Anthropology – Jean-Paul L. Garnier

Chapbooks

Shelf Life – F. J. Bergmann

Mars Maundering – Denise Dumars

The Telepathy Machine – Jean-Paul L. Garnier

Time's Arrow – Jean-Paul L. Garnier

Utopian Problems – Jean-Paul L. Garnier

www.spacecowboybooks.com

Another Time

Time Travel Stories

edited by Jean-Paul L. Garnier

ISBN 978-1-7328257-9-6

Edited by Jean-Paul L. Garnier
Book design by F. J. Bergmann
Cover image by Zara Kand

First Edition | 2024

Space Cowboy Books
61871 29 Palms Hwy.
Joshua Tree, CA 92252
www.spacecowboybooks.com

Contents

Introduction: Ages of Absurdity

It takes an author made of stern stuff to write a time travel story.

Thankfully, it does *not* take an author made of stern stuff to write the introduction to an anthology of time travel stories—so here I am.

Change one thing in such a tale: a particular line of dialogue, the meeting of characters, the ordering of events—and the narrative inevitably dissolves into nonsensical paradox, a point from which, no matter how much you tinker with it, the entire center collapses. The challenge comes from having to be one step ahead of the reader, with an eye on how the denouement of the story you're trying to tell returns—or perhaps ruptures—its opening premise. To write a time travel story, and have it *remain* coherent, continuous, yet compelling—is itself to become a time-traveler, perhaps more so than in any other sub-genre of SF.

This is not the place to outline the various flavors of ontological schism that can occur when laws of causality are broken. Rather: it is, but through the selection of works by pioneering souls of Golden Age-ish science fiction, expertly curated by Jean-Paul Garnier. In the collected stories that make up this volume you'll find protagonists trying to prevent their own murders, utopias, meddling extraterrestrials, trombone players, mysterious elements that bring about a deadly plague, and many other time-tangled phenomena.

I say Golden Age-*ish* (this is also not the place to reopen the old arguments about SF's periodization) because these stories are notable in their publication dates that span the 1940s and 1950s: a period that saw the cataclysm of a second world war, the casualties of which included many notable periodicals of the genre. The twin traumas of mass, mechanized warfare and the visceral reality of nuclear annihilation understandably affected the kinds of stories writers told about the future; writers had "lost faith" in it, finding themselves, in the decade leading into the radical experimentalism of the 'New Wave,' inhabitants of a world growing "more irrational, more absurd."[1] The solution? To do what science fiction has always done: to meet and amplify and celebrate that absurdity with irrational narratives that embrace it, full-bodied.

The names gathered in this volume include the familiar (Henry Kuttner, Anthony Boucher, Alfred Bester) and the more obscure, and while anxieties of futurity certainly drive many of their plots, there is a refreshing comic sensibility at play across the anthology—not to mention a playful mirror of the "absurdity" found in their contemporary societies. Irrationality and absurdity, it seems, are constant coordinates across the space-time continuum.

Garnier kicks things off with a bang. The avian aliens of C. Shook's "The Band Played On" are a thrilling pleasure to encounter—if not for the bemused and terrified trombonist who finds himself in their dimension thanks to a particularly novel form of time travel! The unfortunate fellow in Darius John Granger's "Stop, You're Killing Me!" struggles to escape the inexplicable attempts of his wife and son to murder him, and becomes tasked with destroying a time machine to free a future ancestor from his "barbaric age." One of many humorous tales in the anthology, the story also features another smart, and not overly cute, twist. Evelyn E. Smith's "The Man Outside" deploys a Terminator-esque plot (I can make that comparison, even though forty years separate the texts: we're in the time paradox, baby!) about a man whose time-traveling ancestors return to keep him alive and safe from the assassination attempts of a supposedly nefarious cousin, "Conrad." The denouement is both genuinely startling and makes complete, retrospective sense. I guarantee you won't see the ending of this story coming. Just like the protagonists.

---

1. Thomas D. Clareson, "Toward a History of Science Fiction," in *The Science Fiction Reference Book*, ed. Marshall B. Tymn (Washington: Starmont House, 1981), pp. 3–19, p. 14.

Next is Sylvia Jacobs' "Time Payment": a story whose characters insist does not feature a time machine, rather, a "metachronoscope." I won't say too much more about it—go read it yourself, now, immediately. (Yes, you can start with the fourth story of the anthology. Is this or is this not an anthology to do with time travel? Break free of the shackles of spatio-temporal linearity!) Suffice it to say: what starts as just another science fictional romp, in tone, becomes something far more original—and disturbing.

Murder—or the prevention of—is a common theme in the anthology that plays out in particularly startling fashion in Rog Philips' "Repeat Performance," which follows another harried protagonist as they desperately try to influence a future they wish to live to see. In "Time Out For Redheads," Mikel Skot sees a woman murdered before his very eyes, and flees through time, via the apparatus of the time travel tourism company he works for. Who murdered the woman—and for what reason—you'll never guess. Anthony Boucher's "Transfer Point" takes a somewhat metatextual approach to the theme, and incorporates some of the most creative aliens I've seen in short fiction.

Henry Kuttner's "Noon" manages the extraordinary task of holding both localized and species-spanning concepts of time in synchrony, replete with haunting imagery that invokes the inexorable extravagance of dream-logic. It also takes many disparate SFnal elements (a floral, utopian planet, AI, titanic humanoids, damsels distinctly *not* in distress) and unites them in a narrative that is moving, coherent, and true. Garnier closes out the anthology with Alfred Bester's "The Unseen Blushers": an appropriately metafictional tale that lampoons the concept of "creative genius in American letters," with another twist ending that proves an unexpected delight.

If you've ever read an anthology edited by Garnier you know you're in good hands; you don't need me to confirm it. But, regardless, I want to end this introduction by tipping my hat to the editor. If it takes stern stuff to write a time-travel story—

it certainly takes mettle to compile an anthology of them. The anthology you hold in your hands—or read on your screens, or project through your speakers, or are currently beaming directly into your anterior insula, or … —is a collection of stories that take an old and familiar concept, and render it in ways that are fresh, undated, and surprising to a twenty-first century reader.

May these stories stay as fresh, and undated, and surprising, in the centuries to come.

—*Dr. Phoenix Alexander*
Riverside, CA
September 2023

PHOENIX ALEXANDER is a queer Greek-Cypriot writer and curator of science fiction, fantasy, and horror. His work has appeared in publications including *The Magazine of Fantasy and Science Fiction*, *Beneath Ceaseless Skies*, *Escape Pod*, *The Deadlands*, *Science Fiction Studies*, and others. He is a full member of the Science Fiction Writers Association (SFWA) and Horror Writers Association (HWA) and served as a judge for the Arthur C. Clarke Award for 2021 and 2022. A fashion designer by training, he completed his PhD at Yale University, and in his day job serves as the Jay Kay and Doris Klein Librarian for Science Fiction and Fantasy at the University of California, Riverside, where he curates one of the world's largest catalogued collections of science fiction.

The Band Played On

C. Shook

Originally published in *Astonishing Stories*, June 1942

'M PLAYING TROMBONE in a little five-piece combo at Benny's Bar and Grill when it happens. At the time we are slightly enlarged by the presence of four of Bill Gundry's boys who are working out at the park and have dropped by to sit in after they have finished, and also we have present Eddie Smith and Mart Allen, who are a clarinet and trumpet from The Pines.

Benny's is the local hangout for all the musicians in town, which is the main reason I'm playing there; one night Whiteman himself shows, when his band is working a theatre job at the Palace.

During the early part of the night we play our own arrangements off the paper, but after about one o'clock we are liable to be jamming with any of the boys who can find seats—like this night I'm telling you about.

When I first notice it we are giving out on the "Jazz Me Blues," which is a fine ensemble number, and we are hitting it in a fast Dixieland. I'm ragging the beat and I can feel the old slush pump tremble, but I figure it's because I'm really solid at the moment and I keep on sending.

Well, we clean up the "Jazz Me's" and I'm still hot so I hit right on the B-natural for "Stardust," with the boys jumping in, and we take it slow and mellow through one chorus together. Then I stand up for a solo on the second, and that is when it happens.

I don't know exactly what takes place, but I'm riding as I reach out for a high one that's really out of the world. I feel the pump tremble again, and then what happens is that I am really out of the world.

I mean *I'm actually out of the world!*

The vibrations from the trombone shoot right up my arms, and then my whole body is shaking. I can't stop it. The lights fade away and I'm trembling so I can't even hear the music ... and then I'm not shaking any more, but Benny's is not there or I'm not there, and it is daylight, which is crazy because it is only two AM.

I am still kind of weak as I look around, and then I'm weaker still. The least thing, I figured, was that I had had a spasm or something and was in a hospital and it was the next day. But when

I look around again I know this is no hospital. I'm lying on a big flat rock and I am dressed just as I was at Benny's. I even have my slip-horn beside me.

But the thing that gives me the jumps is the grass. It is all purple. And the trees and everything around have purple leaves where they should be green. I look at my coat. It is a light blue. My pants are black and my skin is white. Then I look at the grass beside me. I reach out and pick a handful. It is plenty purple all right. And I'm thinking as I look at it there in my hand that there is no place in the world where the trees and plants are purple. No place in the world....

I know I am not asleep, but tell myself, "Whenever you read about anything like this happening, the hero always thinks he is asleep at first and pinches himself to find out whether he is or not." So I reach over for my slush pump and give it a good blast. I hear it all right. Just to make sure, I do pinch myself lightly, but it is no soap. I am here and the grass is still purple. I get up off the rock and walk about.

When I stand up I find that I am in a large meadow with nothing more in sight than the rocks here and there and a few trees. The purple grass is nearly knee-high. There is no sense in staying where I am, so I pick up my trombone and begin hiking. After I have walked a couple of miles, maybe, I come to a river. I am not surprised to find that the water is a deep yellow. Nothing will surprise me now.

There must be some settlement along this river if there is anyone living around here, I figure, so I follow along the way the water is flowing. Three or four hours I tramp, and this is something I am not used to. My feet are getting plenty beat and I take up the old bleater and try "The Stars and Stripes Forever," the only march I can think of. This helps me stumble along in two-four time a while, but it uses up what wind I have left, and pretty soon I am forced to sit down and rest.

Well, I guess I doze off while I am resting, for when I come out of it I find myself tied up tighter than a drum, and there in front of me are four men or animals or something examining my trombone.

"Hey," I say.

At that they turn around and stare at me and I stare even harder at them. And then I bust out laughing. For they look like four grown up Donald Ducks. They have duck bills for mouths, and their feet are webbed, but they have arms instead of wings. Their bodies are covered with feathers, except for their heads which have a greenish skin and would almost be human if it weren't for those bills and the green color.

They begin to gab among themselves and I am surprised because I am expecting to hear them quack like ducks. Their voices are low-pitched and they talk way down in their throats something like German, but though I don't understand it, I know it isn't. They are talking about me, I can tell, and finally one of them comes over and unties my feet and legs. But he leaves my arms fastened. He motions for me to get up. I do and we start down the river with one of them carrying my slip-horn and walking beside me, and the others floating on the water like their barnyard relatives. This is the way we come to their town.

It is only a short distance before the river widens considerably, and I can see that it is dotted with little islands. The three men who are swimming come close to shore and they walk with the one guarding me, pointing out at one of the islands as they speak. I gather that they don't know how to take me out there. One of them gestures at the water and then at me, but I shake my head no. They gab some more.

Finally one of them hops into the water and swims to the nearest island. He is back in a flash with about ten other duck men who immediately begin gabbing excitedly as soon as they see me. The one holding my trombone says something to them and they shut up and get back into the water. They push me to the edge of the bank and then one of them takes hold of my legs and pulls me into the river on his back. He almost sinks before the others can grab me too and help him out, and even at that they are as far down as low

E on the doghouse when they start out for the large island almost in the center of the river. This must be their main village, I figure, and it turns out that I am right. Once we get to the village they untie my arms and hand me my horn. I guess they figure I can't get off the island now.

∞

WELL, I DON'T KNOW what I'm in for, but whatever it is, it is postponed for a while because they take me to a small hut and leave me. There is nothing in the hut except a pile of pale purple straw in one of the corners, but I don't need anything else. I am plenty weary and I flop on the straw and am asleep in a minute.

When I awake again, it is morning. I get up and walk to the door and there are four or five of the duck men standing nearby. They see me come out and they smile, but when I start to move about, they point back into the hut and so I go back in and sit down. I am still sitting there when some others come in with some trays of food. These are a lot lighter green in the faces and I guess they must be the women of the race. They have a lot of stuff that looks like purple lettuce, and different vegetable-looking things on the trays, and they act as if I am to eat them. After I taste them they are not so bad. I even drink a cup of the yellow water, and it is not so bad either, only sweeter than I would want ordinarily.

Once I have finished, I go back outside. Right in front of the door is the duck man which carried my slush pump on the walk yesterday, and when he sees me he smiles and comes over and hits me on the back with his hand. I do the same to him and he smiles wider. This means we are friends, I figure, like shaking hands, so I smile too. He motions for me to come with him.

Some of the others come with us, and we walk all around the village which is not so large. My friend seems to be the head man. He walks with me, and the rest stay a little behind. I am being treated like I have the key to the city. All around are the small huts like the one I slept in, and there isn't much else to the town except for a couple of larger buildings which are made of the same purple wood that the huts are made of. I figure that if three people occupy each hut, there are maybe six hundred altogether in the town. There are some other villages on the islands I can see, but they are not so large.

After we have toured for an hour or two, the chief takes me to one of the large buildings and we go inside. City hall, I think. And sure enough we go right to the mayor's office, which is a little room partitioned off from the rest. There are a couple of stools or something there, and the mayor hops up on one with his thin legs underneath him. I sit on the other. He smiles and I smile, and I think this is getting pretty dull and maybe it would be better if he weren't so friendly because anyway I would have some action. I think I will get away and go over and try a few numbers on the horn.

Finally after we sit there smiling for some time, he points to himself.

"Ogroo," he says. His name.

So I hit myself on the chest and tell him my name.

Then he walks around the room and points to the stools and the table and the walls. He says words at each one. He is trying to teach me their language, so I repeat each one after him. We play this little game for quite a while and then we have food brought in. While we are eating, Ogroo is telling me the name of what I am chewing on and it doesn't taste nearly as good as it did when I knew it was plain food only.

When we finish eating, Ogroo gets up and takes me back to our hut. I am supposed to stay there, I see. Anyway I think I will get out a few riffs just to keep in practice, so I go inside for my slush pump. It isn't there.

So this is why the so and so was keeping me away all the time he did, I say to myself. I am plenty burned up, but there is nothing I can do.

When Ogroo shows up the next morning, I try to tell him about it, but he pretends not to understand. Instead we go through the same routine as the day before, only we eat in another room and he shows me some new words.

∞

WELL, THE HORN DOESN'T show up and I can tell my lip is slipping out of shape. It is now three weeks since I got into this place and I have nothing different. I am able to talk to the duck men, though, and I will say for Ogroo that he is a good teacher since I am never more than a poor C in languages when I am in school.

And then one day Ogroo says to me, "Mac, I am happy to tell you that we have located the object which you call a trombone. One of the men took it and has had it hidden. He feared it was a thing of evil power. I assured him it was not, though I was not so sure myself. I hope that I was correct."

"Ogroo, old boy," I tell him, "the trombone is strictly a thing of good power as I will show you if you will produce it. It is a thing of music."

"Why, Mac," says Ogroo, "why did you not say this before. We have music too. It is our great pride."

∞

NOW DURING THE TIME the mayor has been educating me, there is one of the large buildings which I have never been in. I have asked Ogroo about this and he has always said they were saving it as a surprise for me. But now he gets up and starts out the door.

"You will know of the surprise at last," he says.

And he leads me to the big barn which has always been closed.

Well you can hang me for a long-hair when we get inside, for there are about two hundred of the duck people shuffling around like a flock of jitterbugs, and ten or twelve players are giving out with some corny rhythm on a raised platform for a bandstand. They have about three-fourths percussion, mostly tom-tom-like drums, but there are a few gut buckets of some kind which they do not appear to play for nothing.

Ogroo looks at me.

"Is it not magnificent?" he says.

"Well," I say, "it is all right, but where I come from it is done in a slightly different manner. I shall be happy to show you if you will kindly produce my horn."

I can hardly wait to lay my lip into a solid beat the more I listen to these ickies peeling it off the cob, and when one of the men finally brings in old Susie, I kiss her lovingly. She is in fine shape.

Old Ogroo stops the noise. He makes an announcement, and everything is quiet as I step up with my slush pump. It is like Goodman at Carnegie Hall.

Everybody crowds around as I give out with the "Royal Garden Blues." I see I have them overcome and I begin to send softly as I hear one of the boys pick up the beat in the background. He is not so awful at that. After I have taken two choruses, one of the gut buckets has picked up the melody and I dub in the harmony for him. The crowd is beginning to sway slightly when I slide into "Rose Room" and pretty soon they are on the jump until it is worse than a bunch of the alligators at a Krupa concert. All in all it is a very successful performance indeed.

By the time I have finished, I see that I have first chair cinched, and the crowd is eating out of my hand.

This is by no means the last performance I give. I soon have the duck men in the band playing the best jive they can give out with, but it is rather sorry without any reeds and only one brass. They are entirely unable to play any wind instruments, though, so I am forced to make the best of it.

We play for three or four hours, and when old Ogroo and I finally leave the hall, I am cheered all down the line. I am really terrific.

"Mac," Ogroo tells me when we are outside, "you are wonderful. We appreciate music and in fact it is the biggest thing in our lives here. But you are lucky that we are the ones that found you on your arrival and not the animal men from the woods. They are very ignorant, and your trombone would have meant nothing to them."

Well, this is the first time I have heard about these animal men, and I figure maybe they are a little closer to civilization than Ogroo thinks. I ask him about them.

"They are our enemies," he says, "and are much stronger than we. They control all the land surrounding us, but on the water we have the best of them and they never try to attack us here. However we must venture into the forests sometimes, and then we are in constant danger. Many of us are killed or captured each year."

I think no more about this, however, and I spend my time playing for the concerts they have every day. I am very popular with one and all. But a few weeks afterwards, Ogroo asks me to join one of their expeditions into the forests.

"We have to gather our monthly food crop," he says. "And everyone in the community has to do his share. As you are now one of us, it is only fitting that you come along."

Well, of course I clap Ogroo on the back and tell him I will be very pleased to go, and, in fact, I am not worried much about their enemies because I am a good hundred pounds heavier than any of the duck men and I figured I will be plenty for these animal people to handle. As it turns out, I am right in this respect, but I hit one bad note which almost costs me my life and very possibly does so for my friends.

There are about twenty of us that start out. Each one is carrying two large baskets made out of the purple reeds which grow in the swampy lowlands of the islands. Before we begin, I tell Ogroo that I will swim over if he will carry my baskets, but he does not understand what I mean until I dive into the river and demonstrate. This exhibition is a great surprise to everyone, as they have never seen anything like it before. When I have climbed out on the other bank, the rest of the party jumps in and floats over rapidly. Then we begin walking toward the deep purple forests.

We hustle around all morning, and there is no trouble. What we are gathering is some kind of mushroom that grows around the foot of the trees, and we are looking for certain vegetables which have to have the shade to amount to anything. It is in the afternoon shortly before we are ready to depart that one of the men who is acting as a lookout gives the alarm. There is a group of animal men hunting in the woods and they have spotted us. I am curious to see how these men appear and I hang back some while the others run as fast as they can on their webbed feet toward the river; they are luckily near the water, for they could never outdistance these land people.

Well, I know I can catch up, so, as I say, I wait a couple of seconds. But when I have a gander at our enemies, I am off faster than a sixty-fourth beat, and it is none too soon. As a matter of fact, it is a wonder that I am able to run at all, for what I see charging at me is about ten big two-headed monsters running on four legs sometimes, and sometimes on two. They are not quite as large as a man when they stand up, but they are enough to send me heading for the river. I dive in just before they get there and I am churning the water like the *Queen Mary* when I hit the island. Then I look around to see what has happened. The monsters are lined up at the edge of the river watching us, but they do not try to cross over. They are pointing at me and acting excited, and Ogroo laughs.

"They have never seen anything like you," he says. "But we are safe now, for they cannot—what did you call it—swim?"

I say that is very lucky indeed, as they are remarkably tough-appearing babies, but we do not bother any more with them and pretty soon they have disappeared into the forests. It is over a week later that I realize the bad note I hit and what it is going to do to us.

I AM SITTING ON A ROCK near the island's edge this morning trying to work a little oil out of some plants I have found. I wish to apply some of this to my slip-horn, as the action is getting somewhat gummy and I have neglected to bring any of these necessities with me when I rode out of Benny's. While I am doing this, I see some of the animal men come out of the forest and start toward the river. This is odd since I am told they never do this. They do not see me so I stay where I am, and I see two of them talking and arguing with the others. These two seem to have some idea, and the rest are telling them no and shaking all their heads to do it. It must be a real argument, I think, with two mouths to speak with at the same time. I wonder if one of these animals could get two-part harmony with a pair of trumpets, but then I recall that they are strictly ickies, as old Ogroo has explained to me.

So I watch them some more, and pretty soon the two who are talking most jump right into the river and begin to throw their legs up and down and flail their arms, and they are soon moving across the water just as if they could swim. In fact they are swimming, and this excites me greatly since Ogroo has said they could not do this. I get up quick and begin to hunt Ogroo and luckily I find him right away. I tell him what is taking place and he is also greatly excited.

"I'm afraid we have done it now, Mac," he says to me as we run back to where I saw the animal men. "Those creatures are highly imitative—it is the only way they seem to gain any new skill—and they must have been thinking over what they saw when they watched you swim away from them last week."

By the time he has told me this we are back where I have left my trombone, and are just in time to see the last of the group jump into the river. They are able to make the nearest island, which has a small village of maybe fifty people. Well, I do not like this part of my story much and I will cut it short. What happens is that the animal men wipe out that little village in ten minutes and right before our eyes. The animals are extremely happy and we see them grinning with their ugly double faces as they return to shore.

"Quick," says Ogroo, "we have only a little time. They will bring the rest of their tribe immediately and attack all the rest of our islands. We must hide."

I grab my horn and we hurry to notify our own village. But we are stopped. There is no place to go.

Then we hear the menacing roar of the animal men. As we turn, they can be seen jumping into the river one by one. There are hundreds of them.

I turn resignedly to Ogroo. I start to tell him that we must get something to defend ourselves with, but the people are so paralyzed with fear that I know we can never do it. And then before I can say anything, I see the villagers coming slowly toward Ogroo and me. They seem very angry indeed.

Ogroo speaks hurriedly. "They are after you, Mac. You're the one that showed the animal men how to swim and they are after you. In the state they are in, you will probably be killed. I'll try to reason with them, but it is almost certain to be useless, for they might even be after me. I have been your sponsor."

He claps me on the back and then starts toward his people. I do not know what to do. I can see a detachment of the animal people not more than a hundred yards off shore, and the duck men are moving angrily toward me not much farther away. I see them push Ogroo aside as he begins to say something to them.

I move my trombone nervously. And suddenly I see my only chance. I am shaking before I start, but I fit the mouth-piece to my lip and begin to blow. I take a fast scale and I hit the B-natural for "Stardust" at least an octave higher than it was ever played before. I have got to ride high and fast.

Well, I close my eyes and I am shaking so that I hardly notice the vibrations of the horn begin, but when I reach the E in the third measure, I know I am feeling what I felt in Benny's. So I keep pushing it, and the last I remember I am trying to reach the high C closing.

That is when I pass out....

WHEN I COME TO this time, I am almost afraid to open my eyes. My ears are still buzzing, and I am just beginning to realize weakly what has happened when I hear voices around me which are not part of the score. They are speaking in English. I open my eyes then, and look around.

I find that I am surrounded by a crowd of people who are saying to one another to give him air and to take it easy, and I perceive that I am on a city sidewalk, and in fact, as I look up, I see that it is somewhere on Fifty-Second Street. A perfect landing for a tail gate artist, I think as I sit up.

∞

WHEN THE CROWD SEES me do this they move in even closer, all the time telling one another to give me air, but finally one of them claims that he is a doctor and he helps me up and I go with him and another man in uniform who is probably a policeman. They tell me that they are taking me to a hospital, and I do not remember much after that. When I wake up again, I am in the hospital.

A doctor has hold of my wrist, and when he sees me open my eyes he says, "How are you feeling now?"

I tell him okay.

"Well," he says, "you seem to have had quite a shock, and perhaps you do not want to discuss it now, but your manner of dress and this instrument which you have brought with you have excited my curiosity no little."

I see that my trombone is on the table near him.

"Why no, I do not mind telling you," I say, "though you might find it hard to believe what I have gone through. But first—where am I and what month is it?"

The doctor lets go of my wrist.

"You are in New York," he says, "and it is September of the year Twenty-five O Seven."

"Just a minute," I say, "I must misunderstand you. I thought you said the year was Twenty-five O Seven."

"That is what I did say," says the doc.

"But that cannot be true," I tell him. "Why, I was born in 1914, and it is not possible for me to be living at such a period in history."

He picks up my wrist again.

"You are a little excited," he says, "and I think you had better get a bit more rest. Then we can talk this thing over later."

I see him say something to the nurse who is standing in the doorway all this time, and she nods as he goes out. I start to call to him but I figure it is no use. So I go back to sleep.

The second time I wake up, the doc is back and he has four other men with him. They are sitting in chairs around the room watching me; as soon as they see I am awake they come over to my bed.

"These men are very much interested in your case," the doctor tells me. "I have been telling them about your statement and the strange circumstances attending your appearance on Fifty-Second Street today. Now I feel that you have had enough rest and I want you to tell them the entire story."

Well, I know they will figure I am off the beat, but I start at the beginning and relate the whole story anyway. They do not say a word until I have finished. Then they look at each other and have a whispered session on the other side of the room. Finally one of them speaks up.

"Mr. McRae," he says, "we want to question you a little further if you don't mind. Will you please put on your clothes and come with us?"

I do like they say since there is nothing else for me to do, and when I am dressed they take me down the hall to a big light room which is practically all glass, and they ask me to sit down at a large table.

"Now, Mr. McRae," the first doc says, "I want you to do something for me."

He hands me ten little blocks of different sizes and informs me that I am to place them in the proper holes in a board which he has ready for just that purpose. I do as he asks.

This seems to surprise him, but he is all set with another test, and I spend the rest of the afternoon playing these little games, until I am plenty weary of it and I say so to him.

"Well," he says, "as you likely know, we have been trying to determine your sanity. I will say that you have demonstrated yourself to be entirely normal."

"That is fine," I say, "but now that we have decided that will someone kindly tell me what is this business about Twenty-Five O Seven—and what has been happening to me anyhow."

Another of the doctors answers me.

"There seems to be only one other explanation," he says, "one which we are reluctant to accept but which we must consider if your story is true. You have been in a fourth dimension. The passage of time there is something that we know nothing of, and it is possible that the few months you spent in it were equivalent to the centuries which have passed in this dimension. You have apparently evolved a unique and purely personal method for entering and leaving the fourth dimension, and since it seems entirely dependent on your own physical skill together with a large element of chance, it is of little value for scientific exploitation. That is the pity."

While he is giving out this statement, the rest of the doctors grow very excited, and soon as he has finished they begin throwing questions at him about curvature of space and Neilson's theory and a lot of other stuff which is very confusing to me indeed.

Finally I stop them.

"If you will kindly return my trombone," I tell them, "I will be on my way, as I do not know anything of all this and I would like to get out and see what it is like in Twenty-Five O Seven AD."

"Of course, of course," says the first doctor who is the one who brought me to the hospital. "It is very thoughtless of us. I shall get your instrument and you can come home with me until you are able to adjust yourself to our way of living. It will be a great pleasure to show you what we have accomplished in the time since you can remember, though I must say that none of us has done what you have."

He laughs a little at that, and I figure he is a nice guy, so I say I will be happy to accept his offer.

I go home with him and he introduces me to his wife who is a very nice-appearing female. He tells her all about me and he keeps saying how remarkable it is all the time.

∞

IT IS THE NEXT MORNING when I come down to breakfast that I meet the doctor's daughter who is a very lovely little number of about twenty, and I see that my stay is going to be a very pleasant one indeed.

She says, "Dad has been telling me all about you, Mr. McRae, and I'm going to see to it that you really see the New York of Twenty-Five O Seven. He wants to drag you to a lot of stuffy old lectures and scientific conventions, and exhibit you like a freak, but I'm taking charge today."

I remark that that will be fine.

Well, we start right out, and it is amazing what has been done in my absence. Ann—that is the little number's name—tells me about the change in one thing and another; they are now taking vacations on Venus and Mars, and it is merely a matter of a couple of hours to get to San Francisco or London. Of course this is all very interesting, but I am interested in what they are doing in the musical line. I tell Ann this.

"We are in luck," she says, "for there is a concert tonight up in Albany and you will be able to hear all the finest music there."

"I do not wish to hear the long-hairs play," I tell her. "Let us go down along Fifty-Second Street and listen to a little barrelhouse. That is my racket."

"There is no musical organization on Fifty-Second Street," Ann says. "We do all our listening and looking at concerts like this one in Albany, and it is the only sort of music we have."

By this time we are home, so I ask Ann if she would like to hear how we played it back in the twentieth century. She replies that she would, but not to let her father, the doc, know about it because he is something of a bug on the modern music and considers the old style quite degenerate.

I laugh at this. "What he means by the old style is probably something I have never heard," I say. "You must remember that I am almost six hundred years old, so my style is practically antique. Why, your father did not even know that my horn was a musical instrument until I told him my story, and it is indeed a shame that there are not a few old Beiderbecke platters around so you all could hear what you've been missing."

Well, I have not played the old slush pump since I escaped from the fourth dimension, so I am careful when I pick it up, but after I have tried a few runs I say I am all set. Ann is very curious, and she makes me tell her how it works, as it seems they use instruments altogether different in these concerts we are going to. I explain how the wind goes around and all, and then I move into "I'm Getting Sentimental Over You." I am very mellow, and T. Dorsey couldn't have sounded any better in the little concert I give. Ann is very overcome.

"It is beautiful," she says when I have finished. "Are there words to it?"

I tell her there are, but that I do not know them, so she hums softly as I take another chorus. She has a lovely voice, and I say that tomorrow I will write down the words to some other numbers and let her practice them with me.

When the doctor hears we are going to the concert that evening, he says that he wishes to come along. We get to Albany in about five minutes, so fast that I see nothing in the journey once we have left the New York airport where the doc keeps his plane, and we enter the auditorium in perfect time. As we go in, I am very surprised to see everyone staring at me, since I have borrowed one of the doctor's suits for the occasion and look just like anyone else. And then everyone stands and begins cheering me until I am very embarrassed indeed. I look at Ann and the doctor. They are both smiling.

"You know now that you have become a celebrity," whispers Ann. "We didn't want to let you know right away, but the papers have been full of your story."

So I smile and bow to the crowd, which keeps on clapping. It is very pleasing.

Finally, however, the noise stops and the curtain raises. There on the stage are about thirty or forty musicians, and behind them is a large screen like in a moving picture house. Also there are a lot of electric cords in sight, and I cannot figure what they are for until I notice that each instrument is wired like an electric guitar.

When the conductor comes on, everybody claps a little more, and then he turns to the orchestra. What I hear after that is something I never expect to hear in my life. All those electric instruments begin to vibrate, and on the screen behind them all sorts of shapes and colors begin to flash and then disappear. This keeps up as long as the number lasts.

"You are now seeing music as well as hearing it," the doctor tells me.

"I never saw any like that before," I say. "All the music I've ever seen has been the regular dot variety; do the men play from those flashes?"

"Why no," the doc smiles. "Those symbols that you see are the result of the electric impulse as the musicians strike certain notes on their instruments. They are never the same, and to me they are vastly intriguing. Strictly, it was lousy."

"Oh," I say.

The following day Ann informs me that we are going on a picnic and asks me will I please bring my trombone along and teach her a few songs.

About eleven o'clock we get in Ann's plane, and in no time we are down in Virginia in a nice little spot by a small stream.

"I often come down here," Ann says. "It is one of the best places I know."

There is something that seems awfully strange to me, and I finally realize that it is the green grass of the meadow and the trees, after the icky purple I have been used to for the past few months. I tell Ann about this and about how beautiful the green looks, but I add that it is still not as lovely as she is.

She says that is very nice, and then as I stand up from spreading the picnic cloth, she is standing beside me, so I put my arms around her and then I am kissing her and she is kissing me and it is very pleasant indeed. I see that this is much better than any fourth dimension.

Finally we get around to eating the lunch Ann has brought, and I keep saying how lovely she is, which I also mean. And she is saying I am pretty fine too, and we pass some little time like this.

But after a while Ann says, "Mac, will you play for me now? I love to hear you."

So I say I will if she will sing and I give her the words to "The St. Louis Blues," which I have written out. I hit it soft and easy for one chorus to give her the melody, and then she takes the beat. Well, I have not realized it before, but her voice is plenty schmalz and it is a shame she is not living in my time, for she would be a cinch to panic them anywhere.

After that she does "The Memphis Blues" also, and she has me riding beautifully to keep her up there. She is wonderful.

"You are the one who is wonderful," she says. "I have never heard music like you can get out of that trombone. Play something else, darling, won't you?"

I slip into "If I Could Shimmy Like My Sister Kate," and as I play, Ann moves over beside me.

"Lovely," she whispers.

With that I am really carried away and I hear her humming softly as I modulate into "Tea for Two." I am giving it a real ride, and then I feel it coming over me again. I am in a panic. I try to stop playing, but I can't, and my body is vibrating something terrible.

I dimly hear Ann crying, "Mac, Mac...," as I sink off.

That is the last I can remember....

∞

When I come out of it this time, someone is pounding me on the back.

"Ann?" I say hopefully, but I know inside that it will be useless.

"Beautiful going, Mac. Beautiful," someone is saying.

"What?" I ask blankly.

"That 'Stardust.' Boy, you were really out of the world on that one."

Then I open my eyes and look up. It is Ernie Martin, our sax player, who has the chair next to me in Benny's.

I look around. I am back in Benny's. As I put down my sliphorn there is a scattering of applause from the tables.

Someone shouts at me. I close my eyes, but the noise is still there. I keep my eyes closed, and then I hear music.

Ernie is hitting me with his elbow.

"Get in," he says.

I hear the boys beating out "Rosetta."

"Take it up," say Ernie. "Get hep, kid."

"Me?" I says sort of foggy like. "Oh, no—not me. Leastways not tonight."

I pick up old Susie and walk to the door. I wonder if maybe there's such a thing as being too hep.

Stop, You're Killing Me!

Darius John Granger

Originally published in *Imagination: Stories of Science and Fantasy*, February 1956

IT'S FUNNY HOW a silly little habit can save your life.

I got into the car that morning and was thinking of nothing in particular—except maybe the cases I hoped to be getting downtown in my one-man private-dick office. We live at the top of the city's highest hill, my wife and our son Sam, who's seventeen, and myself. At least it's the highest hill in the residential district and the highest one I know of. So out of habit I patted the brakes to test them as the car began to roll down the slight incline of the driveway.

The brakes didn't hold.

Had I started down Jackson Hill, down the long half-mile slope which levels off at the busy intersection of MacArthur and Houston Avenues, I'd have streaked through the intersection out of control. I don't know what the odds for survival are in such a circumstance, but I'd hate to have to test them.

As it was, I shook my head in surprise and pulled the handbrake, bringing the Olds to a stop at the foot of the driveway. I climbed out and bent down to take a look at the right front wheel. In a few seconds I knew what the trouble was. Brake fluid. There wasn't any. But that didn't make sense because I'd had the car—brakes included—overhauled only last week.

Which meant someone had drained the brake fluid from the Olds.

I checked the other front wheel and it was the same. No brake fluid. I sat there in the car for a few minutes smoking a cigarette before I went into the house to call the local service station and have them tow the Olds in.

It was the third time in less than a month that someone had tried to kill me.

That happens, of course, to private detectives. It isn't only in the movies and the two-bit mystery thrillers that it happens. It happens in real life, too. I know because I've been in the business twenty years. Go downtown some time and look me up; Frank Foley's the name and you'll find me in the Ditmas Building on Pearl Street. Sure it happens to private eyes in real life. They're on a hot case and someone wants them off and because it's known bribes won't do any good, violence, mayhem and murder are tried.

But that didn't fit the situation in this case. There had been three tries on my life. The jets of our gas stove turned on while I was napping over a cup of coffee late of a cold night in the kitchen, with door and windows closed. The pulley of our extension ladder failing to hold while I was up painting the eaves of the house. And now the drained brake fluid.

I was on no important case. All of my work at the moment was routine. They say I am getting old, but don't you believe it. I've got some good cases ahead of me yet. They say I was able to get away with my shady tricks when I was younger but that I'm slipping and can't get away with them now. Don't you believe it. In my business you've always got to get away with them. And when Frank Foley is all washed up, Frank Foley will be the first one to know it.

The situation in this case was worse. The situation in this case was strictly a family affair. All the attempts at my life had been made at home, either by my wife Sue or our boy Sam. Sounds nuts, because we're a pretty happy family usually. But there it was. Either Sue or Sam could have snafu'd the pulley on the extension ladder and either one of them could have turned on the gas jets after I had dozed. As for the drained brake fluid, Sue didn't know a spark plug from the carburetor air intake, but Sam was a hot rod with his own beat-up jalopy and knew as much about cars as anyone since old Henry Ford himself.

I WENT INSIDE and sat down at the kitchen table. Sam was still lingering over his coffee before heading over to the high school. Sue was doing the dishes and humming. She turned around and said:

"S'matter dear, something wrong with the car?"

"You better ask Sammy," I suggested.

"Sammy? But why?"

"I don't get it, Pop," Sammy said still drinking his coffee.

The other two times I had said nothing. Accidents. You don't accuse your own wife and son of trying to kill you unless you're sure. But the drained brake fluid was no accident. I swept Sammy's coffee cup off the table with my right hand and grabbed the front of his shirt. Sue screamed with surprise as I dragged Sammy to his feet.

"You drained out the brake fluid," I said.

"I don't know what you're talking about, Pop. What's the matter with you? You'll rip the shirt!"

"Lay off of him for crying out loud, Frank," Sue cried out.

"Lay off of him," I said, repeating her words and imitating her tone. This always exasperated Sue. She put down her dish rag and came over to me and hollered:

"Well, you haven't said what's the matter."

"I said he drained the brake fluid out of the car. I could have killed myself."

"That's ridiculous, Frank, and you know it. Why would Sam do a thing like that?"

"How should I know why he'd do a thing like that?"

"Why don't you let go of him?"

I did so and Sammy slumped down into his chair. "How should I know," I went on, "why either one of you would bolix up the extension ladder or turn on the gas jets right here in the kitchen while I was dozing?"

"What?" Sue gasped. "What did you say?"

"You heard right, Mom," Sammy said, staring at me as if I'd just escaped from the twentieth century equivalent of bedlam.

"Frank, you've been working too hard," Sue said. "Why don't you take a vacation? We could go off to—"

"Oh, to hell with a vacation," I said, but I was simmering down. They both looked so completely innocent, it kind of stopped me. Add to that fact that my family had no reason in the world for trying to kill me, and I was almost inclined to believe them.

Except that you couldn't change the facts. You couldn't change what had happened.

I turned around without saying anything and headed for the door.

"Why don't you drop in on Doc Mundin on the way to work?" Sue suggested.

I slammed the door and went out to the wife's car and got in and drove downtown. All the way down, you could have threaded a needle with the line my lips made.

THERE WAS ONE CUSTOMER in my waiting room when I reached the office. I offered him a curt nod and went by the inner door. "Be right with you," I mumbled. He didn't respond. He was a short, chunky man with hips as wide as his shoulders and a flabby, loose-jowled face but a chest like a barrel. I gave him a double take when he failed to respond. I said, "Well, do you want to see a private detective or don't you?"

"I want to see you," he said.

Somehow, I didn't like the way he said it, but let it ride. "Be right with you," I told him as I unlocked the inner door and moved through the sanctum sanctorum, such as it is. I smoked a cigarette halfway down before I pressed the buzzer to admit him.

He came in with the bouncy stride to which chunky fat men are prone. He looked straight at me and smiled as if he had known me for years. "I'm glad to see you're still alive, Mr. Foley," he said.

I stood up. "Would you say that again please?" I asked him.

"I'm glad to see you're still alive."

"Just what the hell is that supposed to mean?"

"Well, let me see. By this time your wife and son would have tried three times to kill you. That being the—"

I was around the desk before he could finish. I grabbed him much harder than I had grabbed Sammy. Something—probably the lining of his jacket—ripped. "You'd better explain that," I suggested.

"There's hardly anything to explain. Your wife tried to kill you by almost cutting through the pulley rope of your extension ladder, but you got off with a sprained ankle. She tried to kill again by leaving the gas jets on one night in the kitchen. But you awoke in time. Your son tried to kill you this morning by draining the brake fluid from your car. There now. Does that bring us up to date?"

I was so shocked I let go of him. I sat down and lit another cigarette with what remained of the first. I watched him brush himself off and settle himself in the client chair.

"I can't blame you for behaving like that," he said.

"What the devil have you been doing, living in our attic and spying on me?"

"Dear me, no. But you see, I know. I know all about you, Mr. Foley. I have to know."

"You have to?"

"Now that you have avoided death the first three times, I'm going to hire you."

"To hire me? What for?"

I must have sounded so amazed that my visitor said: "You do hire yourself out as a private detective? Don't you? That is your function, isn't it?"

"Yeah, but—"

"But how did I know? That's a long story. Too long and too involved for you and probably you wouldn't believe it anyhow. Look, Mr. Foley. I would like to hire you. I am an inventor. Your job will be to protect me and my invention against harm—for as long as necessary. Perhaps the rest of my life."

"The rest of your life!"

"Oh, that isn't very long. You see, I die of a heart attack in 1959."

"I'm sorry to hear that," I said. "You mean, your doctor told you you only have three more years to live?"

"My doctor?" the chunky fat man said. "Dear me, no. My great great-great-great-grandchild told me. And he, of course, knows."

"Your great-great-great-great-grandchild," I said.

"Yes, of course. Naturally the dear boy—if you can call a man your own age a boy—is very upset. He's marooned here, you see."

"This—uh—great-great-great-great-grandson is your own age, you say?"

"Perhaps a little older. I never asked him."

"But he won't be born for a hundred years!" I gasped. There was a silence. Then I smiled at my visitor. I had to smile. He was pulling my leg. He did it the best, the soberest way possible—but he was pulling my leg. There would be a place for him on TV, I thought, and said so.

"But I'm not joking," he insisted. "Everything I told you is true, Mr. Foley. Here is what I want you to do. For as long as necessary, perhaps until my death in 1959, I want you to protect me and my invention. I'll pay you a hundred dollars a week for as long as I live, plus expenses."

A hundred and expenses was more than I averaged, but I didn't say that. I said, "What do I have to protect you against?"

"Why, didn't I say? My great-great—"

"Great-great," I said for him, "grandson. Look, jack. You're talking in riddles. Why don't you spit straight out whatever you want to say? Your great-great-great-great-grandson can't possibly want to harm you because, damn it, he hasn't been born yet. Which leaves us where?"

"Oh, but you're wrong. He doesn't want to harm me specifically. He merely wants to stop me from completing my invention. When he discovered I was going to hire you to protect me he decided to kill you as a warning to me. He tried three times and missed three times so I know you're pretty resourceful, Mr. Foley. I'd feel that my invention and I are safe in your hands."

"First you say my family's trying to kill me, then you say your four-times grandson. Well, which is it?"

"Both. That is, my relative employs mental suggestion on your relatives, using them as agents. They have no reason to kill you, do they?"

"No," I admitted.

"There. Then obviously it must be my—umm, four-times grandson, as you say. Will you take the job?"

"I don't know yet," I said. "I'll admit it, jack. I don't know if you're crazy or I'm crazy."

"Why does either one of us have to be crazy? Can't you simply protect me and my invention and—"

"What kind of invention is it?" I asked.

"I thought you would get around to that."

"Well, what is it?"

"I had wanted to wait until it was finished so I could show you. One doesn't simply talk about an invention like mine and expect to be believed."

When I'm puzzled I become arrogant. I guess you call it bluster and often it can see you through pretty rough spots. So despite the offer of a hundred dollars a week plus expenses I said, "Either you tell me all about it, or we forget you ever came here. Understand?"

"I suppose so," he admitted. "Very well, then—"

"Just a minute. You haven't even told me your name."

"It's Haney. Angus W. Haney, Mr. Foley."

"Now what about the invention?"

"It's almost finished," Angus W. Haney said. "At the moment I can't prove to you that it works. Unless you believe my great-great-great-great-grandson really is what I say he is."

"Whoever heard of a—"

"That is crucial, Mr. Foley. Because if you believe he is what I say he is, then you know my invention will be a success. You see, what I am in the process of inventing is a time machine."

∞

THAT WAS ENOUGH for one day and I guess Angus W. Haney knew it was enough. He gave me his card and told me to call him and I said that I would. After he had left, I got out the office bottle— which that winter was bourbon—and poured myself a good hard slug which went down smoothly. It's a hoax, I kept telling myself. It has to be a hoax.

But was it? I guess I wasn't entirely convinced, because Angus Haney had said that his four-times grandson was using my Sue and Sammy—via mental suggestion—to kill me. And that being the case, I decided against going home that night. What the hell, a guy couldn't take chances, not in my business. You learned to be careful or else you left the business in a hurry or they carried you out. So, I'd wait and see.

I called up home and made some kind of excuse, then took a room downtown in the Hazel Arms Hotel. I checked in, showered, and went outside for a good meal. When I returned to the Hazel Arms it was early, so I killed some time at the bar, then went out and took in a movie.

At ten o'clock that evening I went upstairs to turn in. Kind of an early hour for a private eye, I know, but I was bushed and I guess I'm not as young as I used to be. I shut the door behind me and was about to turn on the light when a voice said:

"After you turn it on just walk to the bed and sit down, please. I'm holding a gun on you."

I touched the light switch and the room was bathed in light and I saw him. He was a middle-aged fellow, but trim and well-preserved with dark piercing eyes and hair graying at the temples. He said, "I suppose you know who I am."

I sat down on the bed, shaking my head. He was seated across the room from me in a wing chair, holding a .38 Banker's Special very steadily in his right hand, the muzzle pointing at me.

"No," I said. "Who are you?"

"I am Angus Haney's great-great-great-great-grandson."

By then I didn't even blink. I merely said, "Go on, I'm listening."

"I tried to have you killed as a warning to my relation, Mr. Foley. You see, I don't want to kill him. I can't predict what might happen if I kill him. It's never been done before, killing an ancestor. I might disrupt the whole family line. For example, I might never be born. We couldn't possibly have that, could we?"

"Not if you say we couldn't. What do you want, jack? To kill me?"

"If I had wanted that I could merely pull the trigger, couldn't I?"

"Yeah."

"I'm afraid trying to kill you was a mistake. Angus is determined to go on with his invention anyway. But if I can convince you not to take his proposition, perhaps I'll be able to destroy his time machine before he has time to hire another guard."

"But why do you want to destroy it?"

"Because I'm trapped here in your primitive age. Because I'll never get back to my own time, that's why."

"I don't get you."

"Look. My ancestor Angus Haney invents a time machine. It can travel forward in time, but not back. In my own day I invent a machine based to a large extent on Angus' earlier machine. It can travel back in time, but not forward. I come here, visiting your mid-twentieth century, thinking I can return to my own day in Angus' machine."

"Then why don't you want it built?"

"Because Angus explained to me that I was wrong. The machines are slightly different. I can travel on my own, but not his. He can travel on his own, but not mine. Result, I'm trapped here. Unless—"

"Unless what?"

"Unless I can prevent Angus from completing his machine. If it's destroyed, my own machine would have been impossible because, as I have said, most of my work is based on Angus'. You'll help me?"

"No," I said. "Why should I?"

"Because I cannot stand living in your barbarous age. Because I want to return home to the world I understand."

"Hell," I said, "Angus is as good as my client right now."

"I will give you," the well-preserved middle aged man said, "ten thousand dollars to help me destroy Angus Haney's time machine."

"And win or lose you won't have my family try to kill me any more?"

"Win or lose," he said.

Great-great—I got to call him that because I never learned his name—waited for my answer while I did some of the fast thinking a private dick has to do every working day of his life. When opportunity knocks, a private dick can't pass it up. He won't keep his shingle up long if he does because the work isn't exactly steady. This, obviously, was opportunity. Ten thousand bucks worth. And ten G's in one lump sum looked a lot better than Angus Haney's indefinite hundred a week.

Did that mean I was turning on Angus Haney? Well, it's a cinch I wouldn't have been booted out of the fraternity of private eyes for it, because despite what you read to the contrary in the two-bit shamus books—of noble impulses and motives pure as chivalry—a private eye is for number one and that's the end of it.

"Mister," I said, "you have got yourself a deal. When do I start?"

"You know where Angus Haney lives?"

"He gave me his card."

"Tomorrow. Tomorrow morning. He's working late tonight so he'll sleep late tomorrow. He's putting the finishing touches tonight on the first time machine ever built. In the morning, we destroy it. All right?"

"For ten thousand bucks," I said, "I'd destroy the Taj Mahal."

IT WAS A COLD CLEAR MORNING. I didn't call home because I couldn't face the wife and kid, not for a while. I had accused them of trying to kill me and it was true enough but they had no recollection of it. I still had the wife's car with me, but she could pick up mine at the service station on her own way to work.

I was too excited to eat breakfast. It isn't every morning you start out to earn ten thousand dollars.

I drove across town to the address on Angus Haney's card. Great-great was already waiting for me, and pacing the sidewalk impatiently. The frown lifted when he saw me and you could actually see him relax down to the tips of his toes.

"I can take care of the machine," he said. "You watch for Angus. If Angus tries to stop me, you take care of Angus. All right?"

I nodded and we went around the side of the house, where Angus Haney had planted rhododendron and azaleas. Me, I don't care much for plants—I only know the names because my wife makes such a fuss about them.

"In the cellar," Great-great whispered. "I have a key."

"How did you get a key?"

"In my own time this house is preserved as a museum. I simply made a key from the restored model."

In silence we approached the cellar door. A look at my wristwatch told me it was seven-thirty. If Angus Haney had worked late last night he would probably still be asleep. The job would be a lead-pipe cinch.

I watched my companion slip a key into the lock. In a moment, the door stood ajar and I was peering down a steep flight of bare wood steps. Nodding at each other, we began to go down.

We stopped short at the foot of the staircase. There was someone down there.

"I thought you said he'd be sleeping," I protested, barely forming the words with my lips.

"I'm sure he's asleep—but I didn't know he'd sleep down in the cellar. Apparently he didn't want to leave the machine even for a minute."

Faint light entered the cellar through the small high windows. At first I saw nothing but the usual clutter of basement junk, but then in the far corner beyond the water tank I saw something which didn't belong. Make that two things. First, there was a man asleep on a cot. Second, there was this machine.

For all I know of gadgets, it could have been a super-powered ham radio set. But a ham doesn't come complete with a glass-enclosed compartment big enough for a man.

We stalked across the floor, Great-great pausing to pick something up. It was a length of steel pipe and with it he wouldn't have much trouble demolishing Angus Haney's untried time machine.

This was it. This was my big day. Ten thousand bucks for almost nothing. I looked at the plump man sleeping on the cot in front of his invention. I felt no remorse. His adversary had made a better offer, so what the hell could he expect?

All at once, things happened fast.

Great-great stumbled over something and went reeling across the room. He was so surprised that he shouted, "But it doesn't belong there! I couldn't have tripped over it! It isn't in the restoration, I tell you."

I didn't have time to point out that the restoration might not be quite accurate. Because the commotion woke up Angus Haney.

He came springing off the cot—fully awake and alarmed in the split-second it took to open his eyes.

"You'll have to kill me first!" he cried, moving in front of the machine and preparing to defend it like a mother lion defends her cubs.

My companion ignored him, trying to work around behind him toward the time machine. I advanced straight for Angus Haney.

"Be sensible, jack," I said, "and you won't get hurt. I'm bigger than you are and I know how to fight. I don't want to hurt you, but—"

He turned away from me, though, and lunged at Great-great. I dove at him in a street clothes version of the flying tackle and we went down together. Angus Haney was stronger than I had expected. Or maybe it wasn't that. Maybe he was fighting with desperation. Because the machine meant everything to him.

Well, the ten grand wasn't exactly chicken feed to me, either. If Angus was going to fight back, I had to play rough. I clubbed him across the mouth with my right fist and his lips became a bloody smear, but he kept kicking and twisting and writhing to get at his relative, who stood poised now over the time machine with the length of steel pipe.

"Don't!" Angus Haney screamed, and rolled clear of me. He was on his feet in an instant and wrestling to get the pipe from my companion.

"If I destroy it, you fool," the man who hadn't been born yet said, "I won't build my own version of it and won't be trapped back here in your twentieth century. You can't stop me."

But Angus, who outweighed his antagonist, had other ideas. In the brief time it took me to climb to my feet and reach them, the metal pipe went clattering away across the floor and Angus was wrestling his relative away from the time machine. I grabbed Angus' shoulder and swung him around and hit him. He dropped like a stone and, with a whoop of triumph, my companion scrambled after the heavy metal pipe.

Angus was down but not out. I'll have to say this for him; he had guts. He was on his feet again before Great-great could reach the machine.

I'll never forget that scene. For a moment time seemed to be suspended. Great-great stood poised with the metal pipe at the top of its arc, ready to bring it down with crushing force on the delicate control bank of the machine. Angus seemed to stop in mid-air as he leaped for the pipe. Immediately behind him was the glass-enclosed booth of the machine. Or—and this is important—it was glass-enclosed on three sides. The fourth side was nothing but air.

I caught Angus around the waist and pulled him back. We stumbled away from the machine and then back toward it. Suddenly Angus went limp. It was the oldest trick in the book, but I fell for it. I relaxed my hold on him and, as soon as I did, he became a fury. Something struck the side of my head and the next thing I knew I was staggering toward the time machine.

Just as Great-great brought the heavy metal pipe down.

I staggered inside the glass-enclosed booth.

There was a loud crashing sound.

And then—unexpectedly—a faint hum—a sudden blurry curtain before my eyes—a rolling, seething, billowing mist of white—and a moment of exquisite pain....

And Angus Haney's voice from a million miles away: "You're destroying it...."

Then blackness like the gulf between the stars.

Or between the centuries.

∞

WELL THAT'S THE STORY. I'm telling you everything so you'll understand. I am not—repeat, not—crazy. I'm as sane as you are. Of course my emotional responses to your mental tests are different: I'm from the twentieth century.

I know I can't get back. I know a little more ought to be said about my story. Angus failed to stop Great-great, who completely demolished his machine.

How do I know?

Because you never even heard of a successful experiment in time travel here in the twenty-first century. Simple, isn't it.

I wish I knew Great-great's name. If I knew his name and could find him, he'd confirm my story. I know what you're thinking. Believe me, I am not a paranoid. I …

What's that? His name's Haney, just like Angus Haney? That figures, I guess. George Haney. Well, truck him in for crying out loud. He'll confirm everything I say—

Here he is now.

"Well, Jack, am I glad to see you! They think I'm crazy. They're trying to tell me there's no such thing as time travel, but I ought to know. I come from the past. And you ought to know, because you went back there to destroy Angus Haney's prototype of a time machine so you wouldn't build one yourself, based on it, and be trapped back in my century. Right? Incidentally, Jack, you can forget all about the ten grand, just as long as you get me out of here and convince them I'm not crazy."

He stares at me. He's Great-great, all right. He frowns and says, "I could not possibly be interested. I never saw you before in my life. And obviously, there is no such thing as time travel." He shakes his head sadly and starts to leave.

"Wait!" I cry. "You don't understand. I understand now. Of course you wouldn't know. You wouldn't remember. Because if you destroyed Angus Haney's time machine there wouldn't be any such thing as time travel and you wouldn't have built your own machine. So you forgot. The episode sort of never existed for you."

"I'm terribly sorry I can't help you, fellow." A genuine look of sympathy in his eyes.

"There's no such thing as time travel. For everybody but me. I'm the one guy who proved time travel was possible—before the first and only time machine was destroyed."

He leaves. The head medics confer. I know what they're saying. I'm nuts. Time travel is impossible so I must be nuts.

But we know better, don't we?

THE MAN OUTSIDE

Evelyn E. Smith

Originally published in *Galaxy Science Fiction*, August 1957

OBODY IN THE NEIGHBORHOOD was surprised when Martin's mother disappeared and Ninian came to take care of him. Mothers had a way of disappearing around those parts and the kids were often better off without them. Martin was no exception. He'd never had it this good while he was living with his old lady. As for his father, Martin had never had one. He'd been a war baby, born of one of the tides of soldiers—enemies and allies, both—that had engulfed the country in successive waves and bought or taken the women. So there was no trouble that way.

Sometimes he wondered who Ninian really was. Obviously that story about her coming from the future was just a gag. Besides, if she really was his great-great-grand-daughter, as she said, why would she tell him to call her "*Aunt Ninian*"? Maybe he was only eleven, but he'd been around and he knew just what the score was. At first he'd thought maybe she was some new kind of social worker, but she acted a little too crazy for that.

He loved to bait her, as he had loved to bait his mother. It was safer with Ninian, though, because when he pushed her too far, she would cry instead of mopping up the floor with him.

"But I can't understand," he would say, keeping his face straight. "Why do you have to come from the future to protect me against your cousin Conrad?"

"Because he's coming to kill you."

"Why should he kill me? I ain't done him nothing."

Ninian sighed. "He's dissatisfied with the current social order and killing you is part of an elaborate plan he's formulated to change it. You wouldn't understand."

"You're damn right. I *don't* understand. What's it all about in straight gas?"

"Oh, just don't ask any questions," Ninian said petulantly. "When you get older, someone will explain the whole thing to you."

∞

So Martin held his peace, because, on the whole, he liked things the way they were. Ninian really was the limit, though. All the people he knew lived in scabrous tenement apartments like his, but she seemed to think it was disgusting.

"So if you don't like it, clean it up," he suggested.

She looked at him as if he were out of his mind.

"Hire a maid, then!" he jeered.

And darned if that dope didn't go out and get a woman to come clean up the place! He was so embarrassed, he didn't even dare show his face in the streets—especially with the women buttonholing him and demanding to know what gave. They tried talking to Ninian, but she certainly knew how to give them the cold shoulder.

One day the truant officer came to ask why Martin hadn't been coming to school. Very few of the neighborhood kids attended classes very regularly, so this was just routine. But Ninian didn't know that and she went into a real tizzy, babbling that Martin had been sick and would make up the work. Martin nearly did get sick from laughing so hard inside.

But he laughed out of the other side of his mouth when she went out and hired a private tutor for him. A tutor—in that neighborhood! Martin had to beat up every kid on the block before he could walk a step without hearing "Fancy Pants!" yelled after him.

Ninian worried all the time. It wasn't that she cared what these people thought of her, for she made no secret of regarding them as little better than animals, but she was shy of attracting attention. There were an awful lot of people in that neighborhood who felt exactly the same way, only she didn't know that, either. She was really pretty dumb, Martin thought, for all her fancy lingo.

"It's so hard to think these things out without any prior practical application to go by," she told him.

He nodded, knowing what she meant was that everything was coming out wrong. But he didn't try to help her; he just watched to see what she'd do next. Already he had begun to assume the detached role of a spectator.

When it became clear that his mother was never going to show up again, Ninian bought one of those smallish, almost identical houses that mushroom on the fringes of a city after every war, particularly where intensive bombing has created a number of desirable building sites.

"This is a much better neighborhood for a boy to grow up in," she declared. "Besides, it's easier to keep an eye on you here."

And keep an eye on him she did—she or a rather foppish young man who came to stay with them occasionally. Martin was told to call him Uncle Raymond.

From time to time, there were other visitors—Uncles Ives and Bartholomew and Olaf, Aunts Ottillie and Grania and Lalage, and many more—all cousins to one another, he was told, all descendants of his.

∞

MARTIN WAS NEVER LEFT ALONE for a minute. He wasn't allowed to play with the other kids in the new neighborhood. Not that their parents would have let them, anyway. The adults obviously figured that if a one-car family hired private tutors for their kid, there must be something pretty wrong with him. So Martin and Ninian were just as conspicuous as before. But he didn't tip her off. She was grown up; she was supposed to know better than he did.

He lived well. He had food to eat that he'd never dreamed of before, warm clothes that no one had ever worn before him. He was surrounded by more luxury than he knew what to do with.

The furniture was the latest New Grand Rapids African modern. There were tidy, colorful Picasso and Braque prints on the walls. And every inch of the floor was modestly covered by carpeting, though the walls were mostly unabashed glass. There were hot water and heat all the time and a freezer well stocked with food—somewhat erratically chosen, for Ninian didn't know much about meals.

The non-glass part of the house was of neat, natural-toned wood, with a neat green lawn in front and a neat parti-colored garden in back.

Martin missed the old neighborhood, though. He missed having other kids to play with. He even missed his mother. Sure, she hadn't given him enough to eat and she'd beaten him up so hard sometimes that she'd nearly killed him—but then there had also been times when she'd hugged and kissed him and soaked his collar with her tears. She'd done all she could for him, supporting him in the only way she knew how—and if respectable society didn't like it, the hell with respectable society.

From Ninian and her cousins, there was only an impersonal kindness. They made no bones about the fact that they were there only to carry out a rather unpleasant duty. Though they were in the house with him, in their minds and in their talk they were living in another world—a world of warmth and peace and plenty where nobody worked, except in the government service or the essential professions. And they seemed to think even that kind of job was pretty low-class, though better than actually doing anything with the hands.

In their world, Martin came to understand, nobody worked with hands; everything was done by machinery. All the people ever did was wear pretty clothes and have good times and eat all they wanted. There was no devastation, no war, no unhappiness, none of the concomitants of normal living.

It was then that Martin began to realize that either the whole lot of them were insane, or what Ninian had told him at first was the truth. They came from the future.

WHEN MARTIN WAS SIXTEEN, Raymond took him aside for the talk Ninian had promised five years before.

"The whole thing's all my brother Conrad's fault. You see, he's an idealist," Raymond explained, pronouncing the last word with distaste.

Martin nodded gravely. He was a quiet boy now, his brief past a dim and rather ridiculous memory. Who could ever imagine him robbing a grocery store or wielding a broken bottle now? He still was rather undersized and he'd read so much that he'd weakened his eyes and had to wear glasses. His face was pallid, because he spent little time in the sun, and his speech rather overbred, his mentors from the future having carefully eradicated all current vulgarities.

"And Conrad really got upset over the way Earth has been exploiting the not so intelligent life-forms on the other planets," Raymond continued. "Which is distressing—though, of course, it's not as if they were people. Besides, the government has been talking about passing laws to do away with the—well, abuses and things like that, and I'm sure someday everything will come out all right. However, Conrad is so impatient."

"I thought, in your world, machines did all the work," Martin suggested.

"I've told you—our world is precisely the same as this one!" Raymond snapped. "We just come a couple of centuries or so later, that's all. But remember, our interests are identical. We're virtually the same people ... although it is amazing what a difference two hundred odd years of progress and polish can make in a species, isn't it?"

He continued more mildly: "However, even you ought to be able to understand that we can't make machinery without metal. We need food. All that sort of thing comes from the out-system planets. And, on those worlds, it's far cheaper to use native labor than to ship out all that expensive machinery. After all, if we didn't give the natives jobs, how would they manage to live?"

"How did they live before? Come to think of it, if you don't work, how do you live now?... I don't mean in the now for me, but the now for you," Martin explained laboriously. It was so difficult to live in the past and think in the future.

"I'm trying to talk to you as if you were an adult," Raymond said, "but if you will persist in these childish interruptions—"

"I'm sorry," Martin said.

But he wasn't, for by now he had little respect left for any of his descendants. They were all exceedingly handsome and cultivated young people, with superior educations, smooth ways of speaking and considerable self-confidence, but they just weren't very bright. And he had discovered that Raymond was perhaps the most intelligent of the lot. Somewhere in that relatively short span of time, his line or—more frightening—his race had lost something vital.

Unaware of the near-contempt in which his young ancestor held him, Raymond went on blandly: "Anyhow, Conrad took it upon himself to feel particularly guilty, because, he decided, if it hadn't been for the fact that our great-grandfather discovered the super-drive, we might never have reached the stars. Which is ridiculous—his feeling guilty, I mean. Perhaps a great-grandfather is responsible for his great-grandchildren, but a great-grandchild can hardly be held accountable for his great-grandfather."

"How about a great-great-grandchild?" Martin couldn't help asking.

RAYMOND FLUSHED a delicate pink. "Do you want to hear the rest of this or don't you?"

"Oh, I do!" Martin said. He had pieced the whole thing together for himself long since, but he wanted to hear how Raymond would put it.

"Unfortunately, Professor Farkas has just perfected the time transmitter. Those government scientists are so infernally officious—always inventing such senseless things. It's supposed to be hush-hush, but you know how news will leak out when one is always desperate for a fresh topic of conversation."

Anyhow, Raymond went on to explain, Conrad had bribed one of Farkas' assistants for a set of the plans. Conrad's idea had been to go back in time and "eliminate!" their common great-grandfather. In that way, there would be no space-drive, and, hence, the Terrestrials would never get to the other planets and oppress the local aborigines.

"Sounds like a good way of dealing with the problem," Martin observed.

Raymond looked annoyed. "It's the adolescent way," he said, "to do away with it, rather than find a solution. Would you destroy a whole society in order to root out a single injustice?"

"Not if it were a good one otherwise."

"Well, there's your answer. Conrad got the apparatus built, or perhaps he built it himself. One doesn't inquire too closely into such matters. But when it came to the point, Conrad couldn't bear the idea of eliminating our great-grandfather—because our great-grandfather was such a good man, you know." Raymond's expressive upper lip curled. "So Conrad decided to go further back still and get rid of his great-grandfather's father—who'd been, by all accounts, a pretty worthless character."

"That would be me, I suppose," Martin said quietly.

Raymond turned a deep rose. "Well, doesn't that just go to prove you mustn't believe everything you hear?" The next sentence tumbled out in a rush. "I wormed the whole thing out of him and all of us—the other cousins and me—held a council of war, as it were, and we decided it was our moral duty to go back in time ourselves and protect you." He beamed at Martin.

The boy smiled slowly. "Of course. You had to. If Conrad succeeded in eliminating me, then none of you would exist, would you?"

Raymond frowned. Then he shrugged cheerfully. "Well, you didn't really suppose we were going to all this trouble and expense out of sheer altruism, did you?" he asked, turning on the charm which all the cousins possessed to a consternating degree.

MARTIN HAD, OF COURSE, no illusions on that score; he had learned long ago that nobody did anything for nothing. But saying so was unwise.

"We bribed another set of plans out of another of the professor's assistants," Raymond continued, as if Martin had answered, "and—ah—induced a handicraft enthusiast to build the gadget for us."

Induced, Martin knew, could have meant anything from blackmail to the use of the iron maiden.

"Then we were all ready to forestall Conrad. If one of us guarded you night and day, he would never be able to carry out his plot. So we made our counter-plan, set the machine as far back as it would go—and here we are!"

"I see," Martin said.

Raymond didn't seem to think he really did. "After all," he pointed out defensively, "whatever our motives, it has turned into a good thing for you. Nice home, cultured companions, all the contemporary conveniences, plus some handy anachronisms—I don't see what more you could ask for. You're getting the best of all possible worlds. Of course Ninian *was* a ninny to locate in a mercantile suburb where any little thing out of the way will cause talk. How thankful I am that our era has completely disposed of the mercantiles—"

"What did you do with them?" Martin asked.

But Raymond rushed on: "Soon as Ninian goes and I'm in full charge, we'll get a more isolated place and run it on a far grander scale. Ostentation—that's the way to live here and now; the richer you are, the more eccentricity you can get away with. And," he added, "I might as well be as comfortable as possible while I suffer through this wretched historical stint."

"So Ninian's going," said Martin, wondering why the news made him feel curiously desolate. Because, although he supposed he liked her in a remote kind of way, he had no fondness for her— or she, he knew, for him.

"Well, five years is rather a long stretch for any girl to spend in exile," Raymond explained, "even though our life spans are a bit longer than yours. Besides, you're getting too old now to be under petticoat government." He looked inquisitively at Martin. "You're not going to go all weepy and make a scene when she leaves, are you?"

"No...." Martin said hesitantly. "Oh, I suppose I will miss her. But we aren't very close, so it won't make a real difference." That was the sad part: he already knew it wouldn't make a difference.

Raymond clapped him on the shoulder. "I knew you weren't a sloppy sentimentalist like Conrad. Though you do have rather a look of him, you know."

Suddenly that seemed to make Conrad real. Martin felt a vague stirring of alarm. He kept his voice composed, however. "How do you plan to protect me when he comes?"

"Well, each one of us is armed to the teeth, of course," Raymond said with modest pride, displaying something that looked like a child's combination spaceman's gun and death ray, but which, Martin had no doubt, was a perfectly genuine—and lethal— weapon. "And we've got a rather elaborate burglar alarm system."

Martin inspected the system and made one or two changes in the wiring which, he felt, would increase its efficiency. But still he was dubious. "Maybe it'll work on someone coming from outside this house, but do you think it will work on someone coming from outside this time?"

"Never fear—it has a temporal radius," Raymond replied. "Factory guarantee and all that."

"Just to be on the safe side," Martin said, "I think I'd better have one of those guns, too."

"A splendid idea!" enthused Raymond. "I was just about to think of that myself!"

∞

WHEN IT CAME TIME for the parting, it was Ninian who cried—tears at her own inadequacy, Martin knew, not of sorrow. He was getting skillful at understanding his descendants, far better than they at understanding him. But then they never really tried. Ninian kissed him wetly on the cheek and said she was sure everything would work out all right and that she'd come see him again. She never did, though, except at the very last.

Raymond and Martin moved into a luxurious mansion in a remote area. The site proved a well-chosen one; when the Second Atomic War came, half a dozen years later, they weren't touched. Martin was never sure whether this had been sheer luck or expert planning. Probably luck, because his descendants were exceedingly inept planners.

Few people in the world then could afford to live as stylishly as Martin and his guardian. The place not only contained every possible convenience and gadget but was crammed with bibelots and antiques, carefully chosen by Raymond and disputed by Martin, for, to the man from the future, all available artifacts were antiques. Otherwise, Martin accepted his new surroundings. His sense of wonder had become dulled by now and the pink pseudo-Spanish castle—"architecturally dreadful, of course," Raymond had said, "but so hilariously typical"—impressed him far less than had the suburban split-level aquarium.

"How about a moat?" Martin suggested when they first came. "It seems to go with a castle."

"Do you think a moat could stop Conrad?" Raymond asked, amused.

"No," Martin smiled, feeling rather silly, "but it would make the place seem safer somehow."

The threat of Conrad was beginning to make him grow more and more nervous. He got Raymond's permission to take two suits of armor that stood in the front hall and present them to a local museum, because several times he fancied he saw them move. He also became an adept with the ray gun and changed the surrounding landscape quite a bit with it, until Raymond warned that this might lead Conrad to them.

During those early years, Martin's tutors were exchanged for the higher-degreed ones that were now needful. The question inevitably arose of what the youth's vocation in that life was going to be. At least twenty of the cousins came back through time to hold one of their vigorous family councils. Martin was still young enough to enjoy such occasions, finding them vastly superior to all other forms of entertainment.

"THIS SORT OF PROBLEM wouldn't arise in our day, Martin," Raymond commented as he took his place at the head of the table, "because, unless one specifically feels a call to some profession or other, one just—well, drifts along happily."

"Ours is a wonderful world," Grania sighed at Martin. "I only wish we could take you there. I'm sure you would like it."

"Don't be a fool, Grania!" Raymond snapped. "Well, Martin, have you made up your mind what you want to be?"

Martin affected to think. "A physicist," he said, not without malice. "Or perhaps an engineer."

There was a loud, excited chorus of dissent. He chuckled inwardly.

"Can't do that," Ives said. "Might pick up some concepts from us. Don't know how; none of us knows a thing about science. But it could happen. Subconscious osmosis, if there is such a thing. That way, you might invent something ahead of time. And the fellow we got the plans from particularly cautioned us against that. Changing history. Dangerous."

"Might mess up our time frightfully," Bartholomew contributed, "though, to be perfectly frank, I can't quite understand how."

"I am not going to sit down and explain the whole thing to you all over again, Bart!" Raymond said impatiently. "Well, Martin?"

"What would you suggest?" Martin asked.

"How about becoming a painter? Art is eternal. And quite gentlemanly. Besides, artists are always expected to be either behind or ahead of their times."

"Furthermore," Ottillie added, "one more artist couldn't make much difference in history. There were so many of them all through the ages."

Martin couldn't hold back his question. "What was I, actually, in that other time?"

There was a chilly silence.

"Let's not talk about it, dear," Lalage finally said. "Let's just be thankful we've saved you from *that!*"

So drawing teachers were engaged and Martin became a very competent second-rate artist. He knew he would never be able to achieve first rank because, even though he was still so young, his work was almost purely intellectual. The only emotion he seemed able to feel was fear—the ever-present fear that someday he would turn a corridor and walk into a man who looked like him—a man who wanted to kill him for the sake of an ideal.

But the fear did not show in Martin's pictures. They were pretty pictures.

∞

COUSIN IVES—now that Martin was older, he was told to call the descendants cousin—next assumed guardianship. Ives took his responsibilities more seriously than the others did. He even arranged to have Martin's work shown at an art gallery. The paintings received critical approval, but failed to evoke any enthusiasm. The modest sale they enjoyed was mostly to interior decorators. Museums were not interested.

"Takes time," Ives tried to reassure him. "One day they'll be buying your pictures, Martin. Wait and see."

Ives was the only one of the descendants who seemed to think of Martin as an individual. When his efforts to make contact with the other young man failed, he got worried and decided that what Martin needed was a change of air and scenery.

"'Course you can't go on the Grand Tour. Your son hasn't invented space travel yet. But we can go see this world. What's left of it. Tourists always like ruins best, anyway."

So he drew on the family's vast future resources and bought a yacht, which Martin christened *The Interregnum*. They traveled about from sea to ocean and from ocean to sea, touching at various ports and making trips inland. Martin saw the civilized world— mostly in fragments; the nearly intact semi-civilized world and the uncivilized world, much the same as it had been for centuries. It was like visiting an enormous museum; he couldn't seem to identify with his own time any more.

The other cousins appeared to find the yacht a congenial head-quarters, largely because they could spend so much time far away from the contemporary inhabitants of the planet and relax and be themselves. So they never moved back to land. Martin spent the rest of his life on *The Interregnum*. He felt curiously safer from Conrad there, although there was no valid reason why an ocean should stop a traveler through time.

More cousins were in residence at once than ever before, because they came for the ocean voyage. They spent most of their time aboard ship, giving each other parties and playing an *avant-garde* form of shuffleboard and gambling on future sporting events. That last usually ended in a brawl, because one cousin was sure to accuse another of having got advance information about the results.

Martin didn't care much for their company and associated with them only when not to have done so would have been palpably rude. And, though they were gregarious young people for the most part, they didn't court his society. He suspected that he made them feel uncomfortable.

HE RATHER LIKED IVES, though. Sometimes the two of them would be alone together; then Ives would tell Martin of the future world he had come from. The picture drawn by Raymond and Ninian had not been entirely accurate, Ives admitted. True, there was no war or poverty on Earth proper, but that was because there were only a couple of million people left on the planet. It was an enclave for the highly privileged, highly interbred aristocracy, to which Martin's descendants belonged by virtue of their distinguished ancestry.

"Rather feudal, isn't it?" Martin asked.

Ives agreed, adding that the system had, however, been deliberately planned, rather than the result of haphazard natural development. Everything potentially unpleasant, like the mercantiles, had been deported.

"Not only natives livin' on the other worlds," Ives said as the two of them stood at the ship's rail, surrounded by the limitless expanse of some ocean or other. "People, too. Mostly lower classes, except for officials and things. With wars and want and suffering," he added regretfully, "same as in your day…. Like now, I mean," he corrected himself. "Maybe it is worse, the way Conrad thinks.

More planets for us to make trouble on. Three that were habitable aren't any more. Bombed. Very thorough job."

"Oh," Martin murmured, trying to sound shocked, horrified—interested, even.

"Sometimes I'm not altogether sure Conrad was wrong," Ives said, after a pause. "Tried to keep us from getting to the stars, hurting the people—I expect you could call them people—there. Still—" he smiled shamefacedly—"couldn't stand by and see my own way of life destroyed, could I?"

"I suppose not," Martin said.

"Would take moral courage. I don't have it. None of us does, except Conrad, and even he—" Ives looked out over the sea. "Must be a better way out than Conrad's," he said without conviction. "And everything will work out all right in the end. Bound to. No sense to—to anything, if it doesn't." He glanced wistfully at Martin.

"I hope so," said Martin. But he couldn't hope; he couldn't feel; he couldn't even seem to care.

During all this time, Conrad still did not put in an appearance. Martin had gotten to be such a crack shot with the ray pistol that he almost wished his descendant would show up, so there would be some excitement. But he didn't come. And Martin got to thinking....

He always felt that if any of the cousins could have come to realize the basic flaw in the elaborate plan they had concocted, it would have been Ives. However, when the yacht touched at Tierra del Fuego one bitter winter, Ives took a severe chill. They sent for a doctor from the future—one of the descendants who had been eccentric enough to take a medical degree—but he wasn't able to save Ives. The body was buried in the frozen ground at Ushuaia, on the southern tip of the continent, a hundred years or more before the date of his birth.

A great many of the cousins turned up at the simple ceremony. All were dressed in overwhelming black and showed a great deal of grief. Raymond read the burial service, because they didn't dare summon a clerical cousin from the future; they were afraid he might prove rather stuffy about the entire undertaking.

"He died for all of us," Raymond concluded his funeral eulogy over Ives, "so his death was not in vain."

But Martin disagreed.

∞

THE CEASELESS VOYAGING began again. *The Interregnum* voyaged to every ocean and every sea. Some were blue and some green and some dun. After a while, Martin couldn't tell one from another. Cousin after cousin came to watch over him and eventually they were as hard for him to tell apart as the different oceans.

All the cousins were young, for, though they came at different times in his life, they had all started out from the same time in theirs. Only the young ones had been included in the venture; they did not trust their elders.

As the years went by, Martin began to lose even his detached interest in the land and its doings. Although the yacht frequently touched port for fuel or supplies—it was more economical to purchase them in that era than to have them shipped from the future—he seldom went ashore, and then only at the urging of a newly assigned cousin anxious to see the sights. Most of the time Martin spent in watching the sea—and sometimes he painted it. There seemed to be a depth to his seascapes that his other work lacked.

When he was pressed by the current cousin to make a land visit somewhere, he decided to exhibit a few of his sea paintings. That way, he could fool himself into thinking that there was some purpose to this journey. He'd come to believe that perhaps what his life lacked was purpose, and for a while he kept looking for meaning everywhere, to the cousin's utter disgust.

"Eat, drink and be merry, or whatever you Romans say when you do as you do," the cousin—who was rather woolly in history; the descendants were scraping bottom now—advised.

Martin showed his work in Italy, so that the cousin could be disillusioned by the current crop of Romans. He found that neither purpose nor malice was enough; he was still immeasurably bored. However, a museum bought two of the paintings. Martin thought of Ives and felt an uncomfortable pang of a sensation he could no longer understand.

"Where do you suppose Conrad has been all this time?" Martin idly asked the current cousin—who was passing as his nephew by now.

The young man jumped, then glanced around him uncomfortably. "Conrad's a very shrewd fellow," he whispered. "He's biding his time—waiting until we're off guard. And then— pow!—he'll attack!"

"Oh, I see," Martin said.

He had often fancied that Conrad would prove to be the most stimulating member of the whole generation. But it seemed unlikely that he would ever have a chance for a conversation with the young man. More than one conversation, anyhow.

"When he does show up, I'll protect you," the cousin vowed, touching his ray gun. "You haven't a thing to worry about."

Martin smiled with all the charm he'd had nothing to do but acquire. "I have every confidence in you," he told his descendant. He himself had given up carrying a gun long ago.

There was a war in the Northern Hemisphere and so *The Interregnum* voyaged to southern waters. There was a war in the south and they hid out in the Arctic. All the nations became too drained of power—fuel and man and will—to fight, so there was a sterile peace for a long time. *The Interregnum* roamed the seas restlessly, with her load of passengers from the future, plus one bored and aging contemporary. She bore big guns now, because of the ever-present danger of pirates.

PERHAPS IT WAS the traditionally bracing effect of sea air—perhaps it was the sheltered life—but Martin lived to be a very old man. He was a hundred and four when his last illness came. It was a great relief when the family doctor, called in again from the future, said there was no hope. Martin didn't think he could have borne another year of life.

All the cousins gathered at the yacht to pay their last respects to their progenitor. He saw Ninian again, after all these years, and Raymond—all the others, dozens of them, thronging around his bed, spilling out of the cabin and into the passageways and out onto the deck, making their usual clamor, even though their voices were hushed.

Only Ives was missing. He'd been the lucky one, Martin knew. He had been spared the tragedy that was going to befall these blooming young people—all the same age as when Martin had last seen them and doomed never to grow any older. Underneath their masks of woe, he could see relief at the thought that at last they were going to be rid of their responsibility. And underneath Martin's death mask lay an impersonal pity for those poor, stupid descendants of his who had blundered so irretrievably.

There was only one face which Martin had never seen before. It wasn't a strange face, however, because Martin had seen one very like it in the looking glass when he was a young man.

"You must be Conrad," Martin called across the cabin in a voice that was still clear. "I've been looking forward to meeting you for some time."

The other cousins whirled to face the newcomer.

"You're too late, Con," Raymond gloated for the whole generation. "He's lived out his life."

"But he hasn't lived out his life," Conrad contradicted. "He's lived out the life you created for him. And for yourselves, too."

For the first time, Martin saw compassion in the eyes of one of his lineage and found it vaguely disturbing. It didn't seem to belong there.

"Don't you realize even yet," Conrad went on, "that as soon as he goes, you'll go, too—present, past, future, wherever you are, you'll go up in the air like puffs of smoke?"

"What do you mean?" Ninian quavered, her soft, pretty face alarmed.

Martin answered Conrad's rueful smile, but left the explanations up to him. It was his show, after all.

"Because you will never have existed," Conrad said. "You have no right to existence; it was you yourselves who watched him all the time, so he didn't have a chance to lead a normal life, get married, *have children....*"

Most of the cousins gasped as the truth began to percolate through.

"I knew from the very beginning," Conrad finished, "that I didn't have to do anything at all. I just had to wait and you would destroy yourselves."

"I don't understand," Bartholomew protested, searching the faces of the cousins closest to him. "What does he mean, we have never existed? We're here, aren't we? What—"

"Shut up!" Raymond snapped. He turned on Martin. "You don't seem surprised."

The old man grinned. "I'm not. I figured it all out years ago."

At first, he had wondered what he should do. Would it be better to throw them into a futile panic by telling them or to do nothing? He had decided on the latter; that was the role they had assigned him—to watch and wait and keep out of things—and that was the role he would play.

"You knew all the time and you didn't tell us!" Raymond spluttered. "After we'd been so good to you, making a gentleman out of you instead of a criminal.... That's right," he snarled, "a criminal! An alcoholic, a thief, a derelict! How do you like that?"

"Sounds like a rich, full life," Martin said wistfully.

What an exciting existence they must have done him out of! But then, he couldn't help thinking, he—he and Conrad together, of course—had done them out of *any* kind of existence. It wasn't his responsibility, though; he had done nothing but let matters take whatever course was destined for them. If only he could be sure that it was the better course, perhaps he wouldn't feel that nagging sense of guilt inside him. Strange—where, in his hermetic life, could he possibly have developed such a queer thing as a conscience?

"Then we've wasted all this time," Ninian sobbed, "all this energy, all this money, for nothing!"

"But you were nothing to begin with," Martin told them. And then, after a pause, he added, "I only wish I could be sure there had been some purpose to this."

He didn't know whether it was approaching death that dimmed his sight, or whether the frightened crowd that pressed around him was growing shadowy.

"I wish I could feel that some good had been done in letting you be wiped out of existence," he went on voicing his thoughts. "But I know that the same thing that happened to your worlds and my world will happen all over again. To other people, in other times, but again. It's bound to happen. There isn't any hope for humanity."

One man couldn't really change the course of human history, he told himself. Two men, that was—one real, one a shadow.

Conrad came close to the old man's bed. He was almost transparent.

"No," he said, "there is hope. They didn't know the time transmitter works two ways. I used it for going into the past only once—just this once. But I've gone into the future with it many times. And—" he pressed Martin's hand—"believe me, what I did—what we did, you and I—serves a purpose. It will change things for the better. Everything is going to be all right."

WAS CONRAD TELLING HIM the truth, Martin wondered, or was he just giving the conventional reassurance to the dying? More than that, was he trying to convince himself that what he had done was the right thing? Every cousin had assured Martin that things were going to be all right.

Was Conrad *actually* different from the rest?

His plan had worked and the others' hadn't, but then all his plan had consisted of was doing nothing. That was all he and Martin had done … nothing. Were they absolved of all responsibility merely because they had stood aside and taken advantage of the others' weaknesses?

"Why," Martin said to himself, "in a sense, it could be said that I have fulfilled my original destiny—that I am a criminal."

Well, it didn't matter; whatever happened, no one could hold him to blame. He held no stake in the future that was to come. It was other men's future—other men's problem. He died very peacefully then, and, since he was the only one left on the ship, there was nobody to bury him.

The unmanned yacht drifted about the seas for years and gave rise to many legends, none of them as unbelievable as the truth.

Time Payment

Sylvia Jacobs

Originally published in *Worlds of If Science Fiction*, July 1960

SLICK TENNANT HAD A HUNCH. The sixth sense that had made him king of the local rackets, that had warned him in time when three of his men fell to the machine guns of a rival gang, now told him that the Feds were after him, that they had evidence to send him up for a long stretch. But he was going where even the Feds couldn't extradite him.

Slick Tennant was going to hide in the future.

They didn't call him Slick for nothing. For months, a private dick in his pay had shadowed Dr. Richard Porter, inventor of a device called by reporters a time-travel machine, by comedians a crystal ball, and by Dr. Porter's fellow-psychiatrists a Metachronoscope. Slick knew the doctor was a widower, knew where he lived, knew pressure could be put upon him through Dickie Porter, aged seven. In Slick's pocket was a house-key Dr. Porter thought he had lost two weeks ago.

But Slick hadn't disclosed his intentions to anyone. The chauffeur of his bullet-proof car let him out several miles from the Porter residence. Strolling along the street, Slick might have been any citizen on his way home. A hat shadowed his features as he passed under the street lights, and he carried a briefcase. He hailed a cruising cab and proceeded to a spot two blocks from the Porter home, being careful not to tip too much or too little to attract the driver's attention.

Dr. Porter propped an elbow on his pillow, trying to orient himself in the fuzziness that follows a midnight awakening. He stifled a gasp, and sat up suddenly, as he saw that the man silhouetted against the living room lamp had pajama-clad Dickie by the arm. The child was rubbing his eyes, but there wasn't a whimper out of him.

"I got a gun on the kid," the man said. "I like kids and I won't hurt him if you do what I say."

The doctor struggled to keep his voice soothing and professional. "Of course you wouldn't," he said. "You don't want to go back to the hospital."

The man laughed. "I ain't one of your nuts, Doc. And I don't want your money. I got plenty. All I want from you is a little trip in your time machine."

"Metachronoscope," corrected the doctor. "It's very misleading to call it a time-travel machine."

Letting go of the boy, Slick dealt Dr. Porter a vicious slap. "That'll learn you not to pull none of your high-brow stuff. Is it my fault I had to quit school to keep the family from starvin' when my old man got sent up? If Slick Tennant says it's a time-travel machine, that's what you call it, see?"

"Yes, I see," Dr. Porter said faintly. The mention of gangland's most dreaded name had more effect on him than the blow.

"Now let's get something else straight. Once, on TV, they said a couple of guys came back. Another time, the news program said they couldn't come back and give tips on the ponies. Which is right? Can you bring me back any time you want to?"

"Absolutely not. The decision is irrevocable. The public's impression that the future can be altered or predicted is incorrect."

"Fine. I don't want to come back. And I don't need to change the future, neither. Things may be different, but a smart cookie can always get along. Now, according to the news, you only sent these guys ahead a year. That ain't enough. What's the most you could send me ahead?"

"Theoretically, we could send a subject ahead as much as twenty years, if we could find anyone who would consent to that, and undoubtedly we could learn a great deal more by so doing."

"But you did find out that the boys come through okay?"

"Yes. We sent these two men ahead in 1961. When they returned to awareness, it was 1962. Physically and mentally they were as fit as before."

"Did they know what happened to them?"

"Well, the year had no apparent duration for them, but they had normal speed memories of the intervening year when they returned to awareness. Evidently their fore-memories for the entire year must have been condensed into the brief period they were in the field. From this phenomenon, we derive the term 'sending the subjects ahead' which has so often been misinterpreted. But it's important to note that these condensed fore-memories were not available until twenty-four to forty-eight hours after the events, which means the future cannot be effectively predicted by present techniques."

That sounded like plain English; it sounded as if it meant something, but Slick wasn't quite sure what. He seized on the last remark, which he understood.

"What did you build this gadget for, if you can't tell fortunes with it?" he asked.

"The layman thinks in terms of immediate practical application. But our primary objective was knowledge of the human mind. We confirmed the existence of mental capacities that have been suspected for centuries. We formulated the axiom that awareness is a function of subconscious fore-memories becoming currently available. We experimentally suspended awareness without inducing unconsciousness, by causing the fore-memories to condense. I hope the process will develop into a useful tool for my profession, that we learn how to superimpose conditioning on the blank area to produce rational, socially acceptable action, rather than the literal and irrational compulsion which is a drawback to implanting post-hypnotic commands. But I can't tell you at this point where our research will lead."

This double-talk had Slick going around in circles. But he had a strong hunch that taking a trip in the machine was the right thing to do, and he wasn't going to let Porter divert him from that.

"Let's get down to cases, Doc. Just exactly what's going to happen to me when I get in this machine?"

"It's difficult to explain the process in lay terms, particularly under stress. But this may help you to understand it. Have you ever had the experience of going back to sleep for a few moments after you awoke in the morning, and dreaming a long, involved dream?"

"Sure. I get some good hunches that way."

"Then you know the dream may cover a period of hours, days, or even years. People in the dream move and speak at a normal speed. Yet when you awaken again and look at the clock, you see that only a few minutes or even seconds have elapsed. A motion picture of the events in the dream would be nothing but a gabble and a blur, if projected at such terrific speed."

"Yeah, that's right. I had that happen plenty of times, and I always thought it was kind of funny."

"It demonstrates the capacity of the human mind to function independently of the limitations of chronological time. And premonitory experiences—what you call hunches—give us an inkling of the fore-memory phenomenon. In our dreams, the past, future, literal and symbolical material mingles. But by subjecting the physical brain to a certain type of electro-magnetic field, we can isolate the fore-memories, condensed as in the dream, while the subject acts as if in a waking state."

"Does it hurt when a guy's brain goes into this field?"

"Not at all. Awareness and physical sensations are totally suspended. The elapsing time has no apparent duration. That means you can't feel anything at all, you don't know what has happened until later, and twenty hours or even twenty years pass in a second, as far as your mind is concerned."

"Why in the hell didn't you give me that straight, instead of dragging in all this dream business? That's just what I'm looking for, just what I figured it would be from the news stories. Do you throw this here field ahead or does the time machine travel along with the guy inside?"

Dr. Porter sighed slightly. The man had a preconceived idea, and nothing Porter had said had altered it in the slightest. "The machine doesn't actually travel," he explained patiently. "That's why I objected to calling it a time-travel machine. It exists here and now and it will exist in the future, I suppose."

"You mean it'll be there when I come out of the field?"

"I said I suppose so. Why should that concern you, particularly?"

"Well, I'll tell you. Slick Tennant pays off two ways. Maybe you only heard about the times he paid off guys for crossing him, but he pays off guys that help him, too. I'm paying for your help by giving you a chance to save your skin. I got a hand grenade in this briefcase. When I get through with that machine, I'm going to blow her to little, bitty pieces. Maybe you can't bring me back, but I don't want you to have the machine to send the cops after me, neither. By the time you get a new machine built, my trail will be cold."

Intellectually, Dr. Porter accepted the concept of the inevitability of events. If Slick was going to blow up the machine, he was going to blow it up. Still the old, old human habit of trying to control the future kept obstinately insinuating itself.

"But you don't need to destroy the machine," he protested. "Look, let me try to explain—"

"I thought you'd try to talk me out of it," Slick said ominously. "I know that a lot of money and work went into that gadget, but I got to blow her up. You should be glad you're not on my list or you'd get blown up with her. And I got no time for any more talkin'. I found out all I want to know. Now, get up and get dressed, and make it snappy. You're going to drive me over to the University."

Porter had been careful not to make any moves that might alarm his unbidden guest; he swung his feet obediently over the side of the bed. "Is Dickie going with us?" he asked.

"You're damned right he is. I don't want you high-signing any cops on the way, and the kid might even be sharp enough to phone the station himself, if we left him here." He didn't add that he had an even better reason for taking the boy.

"Then let him get some clothes on, too. It's cold outside." To his son, Dr. Porter added, "Don't be afraid, Dickie. Everything is going to be all right."

"Sure, Daddy," the boy said sturdily.

"You just do like he says. He's like the bad guys on TV."

"You got a smart kid, Porter," Slick said, grinning. "Knows when to keep his trap shut and what to say when he opens it. That's more than some of the hoods in this town know."

∞

DRIVING **DOWN** **THE** **FREEWAY** toward the University campus, Slick and the boy sat in the back seat of Dr. Porter's car. Slick tried the kid on his lap for size; it was a nice fit. The papers said the time machine was a two-passenger job, but if that wasn't the straight dope, Slick could hold the kid on his lap, like this.

The gangster squeezed Dickie's small hand. "You're all right, boy. Plenty of guys a lot bigger than you would be bawlin' if Slick Tennant invited them to take a little ride. If I ever have a kid of my own, I'd want one just like you." He tucked a bill in the pocket of Dickie's jacket. "This is to buy you a play gat or something."

"Thank you, Mr. Slick," the boy said gravely.

Though business compelled him to do things like rubbing out the competition, Slick was really soft-hearted. Some of the proceeds of his illicit activities were devoted each year to buying Christmas trees, turkeys, and toys for poor children. He kind of hated to separate Dickie Porter from his father, but it was the only way he could see to insure a safe passage through time.

And then, Slick reflected, he would have a kid of his own, or at least one he was responsible for. Slick decided then and there that he would send the boy to the fanciest high-class boarding school they had in the future, the kind the millionaire kids went to. Dickie would have a pony, a bike, a dog, plenty of fried chicken and strawberry shortcake, all the things Slick had yearned for in his own slum childhood. He would live in the country, where there were miles of fresh green grass to play on, and he would wear a silver-studded cowboy suit with real spurs. Unless the kids where they were going would be wearing space-pilot suits instead. By gosh, that would be something. Maybe Slick could take the kid on a luxury cruise to the Moon.

To provide these things, Slick would have to follow the only trade he knew, move in on the local mobs. But he wouldn't let Dickie mix with hoods and racketeers. Dickie would study to be something respectable, a mouthpiece or maybe a doctor like his old man. Dickie would have all the advantages a kid could ask for—everything except a real father.

He might even have that, come to think of it. Dr. Porter might easily live another twenty years, now that Slick had warned him to get away from the machine before it was blown up. First, Slick would get some plastic surgery, so Porter and any other old ducks who were still alive wouldn't recognize him. There ought to be a lot of improvements in plastic surgery in twenty years. Probably a guy could even get his fingerprints changed. Then he would hire a private dick to look up Porter.

Slick pictured the aged father being reunited with the son he'd lost twenty years before, seeing the child just as he'd been at the moment of parting, with Slick playing Santa Claus in the background, sending the kid a roll of thousand-dollar bills with a pink ribbon around it for a present. It was such a touching thought that tears came to the gangster's eyes, as they did when he watched a sad movie.

He was sorry he couldn't let Porter and the boy in on his plans right now, but he wasn't ready to tip his hand.

∞

THE MACHINE WAS a two-passenger job, all right. Slick could tell that the minute he saw it. There was no enclosure, just two reclining barber chairs fixed on two circular plates sunk in a platform. After the switch was set, Porter had explained, the additional weight of an occupant of the chair would complete the contact and the field would build up. Slick examined the control panel, particularly the dial, which was calibrated into twenty sections, each for a ninety-second exposure to the field.

"You did say twenty years, didn't you?" Dr. Porter asked.

"If that's the limit," Slick replied tersely, "like I heard."

"How old are you?"

"You mean can my ticker take it? Well, I'm forty-five. They tell me I don't look it." Slick was vain of his black hair, without a thread of gray in it.

"No, you don't look it. But let me take your pulse and blood pressure."

He submitted, without letting go of either his gun or brief case.

"You seem to be in good shape, as nearly as I can tell from a superficial examination. But don't you want to reconsider this twenty-year arrangement? I can't change the setting once you're in the chair, you know. Are you sure you understand that the only thing affected will be your own subjective experience, that time will go on just as it always has, but that you won't be aware of anything between now and twenty years from now?"

"Sure. You told me that three-four times already. What are you trying to do? Stall till help gets here?" Slick asked suspiciously.

"I'm not stalling," the doctor said. "In fact, I'm only too glad to find someone to whom the present means so little that he's willing to go into a twenty-year blank. But ethics insist that I warn you."

He turned the switch to the twenty-year mark.

"I'm ready," he said.

"Whaddya mean, warn me?" Slick snapped. "Is this thing booby trapped?"

"Certainly not. I have merely tried to explain that it is not exactly what you anticipated—"

"You know what I'm drivin' at. Have you got the machine set to electrocute me or explode the grenade? A lot of you respectable citizens don't figure a guy like me is exactly human. You wouldn't call it murder to rub me out. You'd think you was doin' the town a favor."

"Some people would, perhaps, but I'm a doctor, not a judge. I've spent my life trying to find out what makes men like you act as they do, not in devising means of punishing them. But even if I wanted to do you bodily harm, I couldn't. The machine has a built-in safety factor."

This was where Slick sprang a little surprise.

"You willing to bet your kid's life on that?" he asked, picking up the boy.

He took two steps toward the platform, watching Porter's reactions. If the father made a lunge toward the panel, Slick would know the setting was wrong. But Porter only stood stunned. The setting was safe, then, but Slick had only Porter's word that it couldn't be changed after contact. Maybe a change would be fatal to the passenger. So he would make sure there would be no changes.

"I always take out travel insurance. Doc," Slick said, and, stepping onto the platform, he put the boy gently into one of the chairs and reclined in the other himself.

"Dickie!" Dr. Porter cried.

It was the last thing Slick or the boy heard him say.

SLICK CAME BACK to awareness of where he was and what he was doing. He was in one of the radial corridors, but at what compass point, at which level, and how many miles inside the outer walls of the city, he didn't know. He ran his fingers in a puzzled manner through his hair. He had never quite figured out the lettering system of the "circles" which weren't actually circles, but multagons.

He didn't even know what time it was. In this perpetual mock daylight, there was no change; there were no variations of seasons in this sterilized, irradiated, humidified, filtered, deodorized, oxygenated, constantly circulating seventy-five degrees. He remembered when streets used to have names, when you needed a street guide instead of a course in geometry to find your way around the city. He remembered when a city was many buildings, not one immense pyramid, when you wore dark glasses against the sun's glare on the pavements, when a Santa Ana blew dust over everything or smog stung your eyes, when people drove their cars into the downtown congestion instead of leaving them on the outskirts, when they said to each other, "There hasn't been enough rain this year," because there was no weather control and water for the lawns came all the way from the Colorado instead of from the nearby Pacific.

That was the trouble—his mind slipped back to the old days, his memories got out of sequence, and he wandered away from Recidivist Gardens, the only place he felt comfortable and at home. Dr. Tyson said it was because he had been in the field so long that time, twenty years ago.

A young man was staring at him, and Slick looked down at himself. No wonder the young man was staring! To his shame, Slick saw that he was wearing some kind of clothes, and worst of all, he was wearing them inside the city! Where had he found them? The only possible explanation was that he had drawn them out on his museum card. These scrambled-sequence attacks were becoming more embarrassing each time!

"Don't act so flustered, Pop," the young man said. "Nobody saw you but me. Take 'em off and I'll put 'em in the lost-and-found chute for you. Or are you on your way to a costume ball?"

Slick looked over the railing of the balcony. There were several people waiting for elevators and radial cars on the level below, all decently naked, of course, but the young man was right. Nobody else had seen Slick's shame. Hurriedly, he stepped out of the uncomfortable clothes and rolled them into a bundle. The young man took it from him.

"You're very kind—thank you so much," Slick said.

"Think nothing of it," the young man said. "What address should I put on this stuff?"

"Just Recidivist Gardens. They'll take care of it in the office. I hope you don't think all of us at the Gardens do peculiar things like this. It's just that—well, it's a long story, but they didn't start my conditioning until I'd been in the blank five years. I'm not capable of anything really anti-social, you understand, but I get what they call sequence scrambles. Sometimes I act as if I were living in the past. I'm not crazy, though. The doctors at the Gardens assure me I'm not crazy."

"Of course you're not," the young man said soothingly. "But that's a long blank—five years."

"I went the limit, really. Twenty years."

"Then you must be the man they call Slick!"

"You've heard of my case?"

"I was with you the night you made my father put us in the field."

"Dickie Porter! How you have grown! I've always told your father I didn't want to meet you. He said if it was going to happen, it would, whether he introduced us or not. But I hate to face you, after taking such a large slice out of your life—"

"But I'm still young. You're the one who's had the worst of it, because when you come out of the blank, you won't have so many years left. But you have the comfort of knowing you really did something worth while. Your case and mine have been invaluable to the research, particularly yours, because it was with you that my father developed the conditioning techniques. If it hadn't been for you, it would have been very difficult to find anyone willing to draw a twenty-year blank."

"No. Not even a lifer would want that. But I don't take any credit for it. I did it only because I was so bull-headed I wouldn't listen to what Dr. Porter was trying to tell me."

"I came out of it six months ago," the young man said. "Now I can consciously hear, and feel, and smell, just like other people. I don't have to wait till tomorrow to remember what I said to somebody today, or what tonight's dinner tasted like."

"I'm so glad to hear that!" Slick said. "Dr. Tyson says I should be coming out of it soon, too. Say, wait a minute—I heard what you said just now—I'm hearing what I said myself—why, I've had full sensory impressions for several minutes now, but it kind of sneaked up on me—"

The young man seized Slick's hand and pumped it vigorously. "Congratulations! You're out of it!"

"Oh, this is wonderful, wonderful! It's like—like coming back to life. I must go home and tell Dr. Tyson at once! Please go with me. It'll do you good to get out of the city. We're the only two people who've drawn such a long blank—we have so much in common. I'll fix you a chicken dinner. I raise my own. Just think, to taste my own fried chicken!"

"I wish I could go, but it'll have to be some other time. I have a date for the opera. When you see it on the Tri-di-cast you'll know my girl and I are in the studio audience."

"Oh, a girl!" Slick said. "Of course there'd be a girl, now that you're out of the blank. I won't keep you. But there's just one thing I must ask you—do you ever remember ahead? Consciously, that is?"

"A few times. But the conscious fore-memories are mixed with post-memories and impossible to place according to dates. It's the same objection that applies when people remember ahead in dreams—you don't know which part of the dream is a fore-memory until it happens."

"Maybe some day they'll learn to sort those conscious fore-memories out. If I could do it, I would know whether you are ever coming to see me."

"I will come," the young man promised. "Believe me, I will."

Absorbed in his newly found sensations, Slick took the elevator a hundred and thirty-three floors to ground level, reminding himself not to go too far and wind up in one of the sixty levels below ground. Then he stopped the North-by-Northwest radial car and punched the button for city limits, thus avoiding the necessity of dealing with the circle lettering system.

He sat in the speeding little car, watching the faces of the other passengers, until each, in turn, got off at their respective stops. Got off to go to luxurious apartments that were nothing more than cells, with four-sided soundproofing separating neighbor from neighbor, with air, newspapers, prepared meals and all other deliveries coming by chute. How could they bury themselves in the ugly angularity of masonry and steel? How could they, who had always had full senses, deny themselves the sting of wind, the scent of soil and grass, the sound and sight of ocean breakers? How the world had changed in his lifetime, with people who had never committed anti-social acts imprisoning themselves, while those who had needed conditioning enjoyed the therapy of freedom.

When the car reached city limits, the door opened automatically and Slick, the only passenger left, passed through the shower that sprayed his skin with a porous, temporary plastic coating against the chill outside air. He walked across the thick ground-cover, exquisitely aware of the sensation of softness under his feet, leaving the awesome bulk of the city behind.

Before him swept the expanse of Recidivist Gardens, on gently rolling hills, bordering the sea. Clearly though he remembered it, this was the first time he had seen it with full and immediate sensory impact. The moon silvered the foliage, cast a path upon the water. Here and there, lights were on in the cottages nestled among the foliage, the domed, transparent cottages that combined the psychological effect of living outdoors with the comfort of shelter. The sweet note of a bell buoy clove the night.

The beauty was almost unbearable, coming so sharply to long blanked-out senses. The return of immediate awareness, and the knowledge that Dickie Porter, the only human being with whom he had a kinship of experience, did not hate him, was too much happiness for one day. Slick breathed deeply of the salt air, and felt a catch in his heart. He raised a thin hand to his chest.

THE YOUNG MAN who had spoken to Slick in the radial corridor found the obituary item in the newspaper he took from the chute with his breakfast next morning.

> LOUIS G. TENNANT, 65, known to his friends as "Slick," a resident of Recidivist Gardens, died of a heart attack about 2200 last night, while returning to his home after a visit to central Ellay.
>
> Tennant was one of the first recidivists to benefit from the Porter socio-legal conditioning techniques, and was noted for his valuable contribution to science in volunteering in 1963 for a twenty-year blank. He was one of two men who have gone this far ahead, the other being Dr. Porter's son, Richard S. Porter, Jr., level 72, SSE, circle NA, apt. 1722.
>
> The Tennant case did much to direct public attention to the Porter techniques, helping to pave the way for a drastic revision of the criminal statutes, and to establish the concept that punishment rather than treatment for anti-social acts is as barbarous as punishment rather than treatment for the insane.

When informed of the death, and asked whether subconscious fore-memories of these developments motivated Tennant to volunteer as a research subject, Dr. Richard Porter, U.C.L.A., said that the effect of subconscious fore-memories as a compulsion to action is as yet imperfectly understood. He stated, however, that in certain individuals, the fore-memory compulsive factor appears to operate closer to the conscious level than in others. He said that, before going into the blank, Tennant was noted for the strength and reliability of his "hunches." He also recalled that Tennant and Richard Porter, Jr., were the last two subjects treated in the original Metachronoscope, which was destroyed shortly thereafter in an explosion. Subsequent models have been modified and improved. Tennant's estate was willed to the Recidivists' Christmas Fund for Dependent Children. According to Dr. Claude Tyson of Recidivist Hospital, Tennant was still in the blank when he died.

The closing sentence of the item was wrong, Dick Porter thought. In his last hours, Slick had known how it felt to be alive again, after twenty years.

Dick Porter was the only human being who fully appreciated what that meant.

Repeat Performance

Rog Phillips

Originally published in *Imagination Stories of Science and Fantasy*, January 1954

HE POUNDING AT THE DOOR woke me up. I groped for the light. It flooded the room, erasing the glow of the afternoon sun through the drapes. The clock said three-thirty.

"Come on, Benny! Open up!" a gruff voice ordered.

I groaned as I recognized the voice. As I went to the door I hastily reviewed last night's activities. Two wallets on the subway that had netted seventeen bucks, one in an elevator at the Morrison that had added forty-five bucks. An all-night crap game near the Wilson El that had nearly cleaned me....

"Come in, Calahan," I said cheerfully to the cop. "A social visit—I hope?"

Calahan grinned mirthlessly at my little joke. I got dressed.

∞

AN HOUR LATER I was shoved into line with a dozen others. We knew what to do. We walked single file onto the stage, then faced a screen. We couldn't see beyond it because it was dark there, and floodlights from the floor and the ceiling blinded us.

"That's the man!" a woman's voice said excitedly.

My stomach did a flipflop. Who did she mean? Me? I looked at the others in the line-up. Joey North was looking sick. The others just looked uneasy, like I felt. Poor Joey …

On the sidewalk outside the station I lit a cigarette with shaking fingers. I hated the whole system. They take you down in a car. You walk home. If you get out. Suddenly I was sick of Chicago, and when I get sick of Chicago I go somewhere.

∞

NIGHT FOUND ME at the counter in a drugstore in Evanston. I was beginning to feel better. I had a newspaper and a cup of coffee in front of me.

I'd read everything else, so I started reading the society stuff. A lot of it was Evanston. A bosom-type matron smirked at me from one of the pictures. Under the picture it said she was Mrs. Sarah Fish, Evanston society leader. I started to read more. Then this little guy came into the drugstore.

"A package of Camels," he said to the cashier.

He sensed my stare. I looked quickly down at my paper and casually took a sip of coffee. But I wasn't interested in the news now. Out of the corner of my eye I studied the little man. He wasn't more than five feet tall, very slim, and very erect. I got the strange impression of looking at a small giant. Then I realized what caused that impression. It was his head. It was more the right size for a man six feet tall.

"That will be twenty cents," the baldish cashier said.

The little man handed him a bill he had been holding in his hand. "By the way," he said as the cashier rang up the twenty cents, "Could you tell me the way to the Sarah Fish residence?" I pricked up my ears at that.

"Why yes," the cashier said. "You go down to the stop sign and turn right two blocks. It's the big white place set back from the street, with a wide driveway that goes back to a four car garage. Let's see now. That was twenty cents. Twenty-five, fifty, one. Two, three. There you are. Don't forget; the big white house."

"Thank you," the little man said.

I watched him go to the door. It wasn't until he was out of sight that I did a double take.

"Hey!" I said to the cashier. "What kind of a bill did that little guy give you?"

"Why, a—a—Oh good Lord."

I slid out of my seat at the counter and leaned over the cigar counter as the cashier rang up a no sale. He picked out the bill and held it in limp fingers. I took it and spread it on the glass counter.

IT WAS A THREE-DOLLAR BILL. There was a picture of Truman on it. I turned it over. On the back was a picture of an atomic mushroom cloud with a series of ellipses interlocking to form the popular conception of an atom.

It looked like real money. It had the feel of real money.

"Well," the cashier said philosophically. "I guess I'm out three dollars. His talking was what threw me off."

I picked up the three-dollar bill and squinted at the fine print. It said *Series of 1964.* The date on my newspaper on the counter beside my cold coffee was April 5, 1954.

"I'll tell you what I'll do," I said. "I'll give you three dollars for it."

"Oh no!" the cashier said quickly. "I can't do that. The law says I must turn all counterfeit money directly over to the nearest F.B.I. office."

"Sure," I soothed. "Sure, I know that. But this isn't the same thing. A counterfeit is an imitation of real money—and there aren't any real three-dollar bills."

The cashier chuckled suddenly. "By gollies you're right," he said. "That means I can keep it. Think I will. I'm going to deposit it in the bank tomorrow morning. Just for a laugh. Ned Sparks'll fall off his high stool when he sees it."

"I'll give you three and a half for it," I said.

But I was already turning away as he shook his head. I knew the only way to get a three-dollar bill was to catch up with the little man.

Outside the drugstore I looked up the street the way the little man had gone. He wasn't in sight. I saw the stop sign a block away, and hurried toward it.

It was Lincoln Avenue, in a part of Evanston that was just like a small town set off by itself, downstate instead of a northern suburb of Chicago. I followed the directions the cashier had given the little man. Turn right two blocks.

∞

I STILL HADN'T SEEN the little man by the time I reached the big white house with the four car garage. The house itself had one of those old colonial porches with six pillars holding up a porch roof with unnecessary solidity. Between the pillars brightly lit huge windows brought a clear view of the interior.

A party of some sort was going on. That's the way it looked. People standing in small groups holding glasses.

I hesitated. I wanted a three-dollar bill, but was it worth it, to go up to the door and ask for someone I didn't know? I decided it was, and went up the walk as though I belonged there.

Beside the huge door was a button. I pushed it, and heard a series of chimes ring out. A few seconds later the massive door swung open and a middle aged man with a jovial expression said, "Come in, come in. I'm George Wile. Sarah's somewhere. What's your name? Sorry I can't keep track of all of Sarah's friends."

"Ben Smith," I said, stepping inside.

"Sarah'll show up in a minute," George Wile said, and promptly forgot me.

That was okay by me. I stood by the door looking around, trying to spot the little man. A gorgeous young thing held a tray in front of my face until I took a tall glass that contained, I discovered, an excellent Tom Collins.

I couldn't see the little man anywhere. I mosied across the room to the archway to another room where there were more people. He wasn't there either.

A distinguished-appearing man seemed to be the center of attraction here. I edged into the crowd around him and finally deduced that he had earlier given a book review or lecture or something, and this was the refreshment period before everyone went home.

Still no sign of the little man.

Suddenly a sharp rapping sounded. I turned my head. A woman with a large bust was pounding a gavel on the small stand. Around me the buzz of conversation dropped off into silence.

"Is there a Mr. Ben Smith here?" she asked.

"He's here somewhere, Sarah," George Wile's voice sounded loudly. "Where are you, Ben old boy?"

I was too startled to speak for a second or two. Then I said, "Yes!"

Sarah Fish separated me from the crowd with her eyes, then came toward me. There seemed to be concern, a mixture of pity, and something else in her expression. When she reached me she said in a low voice, "Please come with me, Mr. Smith."

No one was paying attention to us. The conversational murmur was on again. I followed her into the front room and around to a door underneath the stairs that arched up to a balcony.

She opened the door and stood aside for me to go in. There was still that strange something in her expression. I tried to place it, then went past her into the room.

The little man was there, standing across the room against a back-drop of shelves filled with books. His piercing eyes flicked at me. Then he lifted his arm and examined his wristwatch.

"Right on the second," he said, a shade of disappointment in his tone. "I'd hoped this time you'd be off a few seconds." He lowered his arm and advanced toward me, hand outstretched politely. "I'm Sam Golfin," he said. "I want to ask you some questions, Benny. And this time I hope I get the right answers."

I ignored his hand. "How'd you know my name?" I demanded. "How'd you know I came here?"

"Oh dear," Sarah Fish said. "I *don't* know how to tell him, Sam. You'll have to."

Sam Golfin gave her a sympathetic glance, then looked grim. "This time," he said, fixing me with a stare, "I'm not going to try to spare your feelings. In—" He studied his watch again. "—exactly one hour and seventeen minutes you are going to be murdered. A man doesn't just get murdered without knowing who might have done it, who his enemies are. Someone in this house is going to kill you. *Who is it?*"

"You see," Sarah Fish said, her bosom expanding in an anxious breath, "you *must* tell us who did it."

I stared at them both, then gave what I intended to be a derisive laugh, but it sounded thin. "What makes you think I'm going to be murdered?" I said.

"For one thing," Sam Golfin said cautiously, "it's in tomorrow's papers."

"Oh, I see," I said sarcastically.

"I know you must think I'm joking...." Golfin said.

"Hardly," I said. And it was the truth. I thought he was crazy.

"I'm glad you don't," Sam Golfin said with relief. "Every minute counts if we are to save you."

"Save me?" I mocked. "But I thought you said it was in the papers. So it must be true."

"I'm not so sure," Golfin said with an important frown. "I'm not so sure the future can't be altered. That's why I'm here. I want to see if I can change the future. If I can...." He left whatever thought he was toying with unspoken.

A sudden thought shattered my amused point of view. That three-dollar bill. It had been a *Series of 1964*, something utterly absurd by itself. But coupled with Sam Golfin's obvious conviction that I was going to be murdered, and his talk of changing the future, it made a pattern that made me suddenly uneasy.

"Why would anyone here kill me?" I asked with a defiance that covered my unease. "I don't even know anyone here. As a matter of fact, the reason I came here was to——"

"But someone here knows you," Golfin said. "And that someone knew you were going to be here. The murder was—will be—carefully planned."

"Just how am I going to be murdered?" I asked, not grinning.

"The coroner's report says that you were—will be—poisoned," Golfin said.

I thought of the Tom Collins, and my stomach turned over.

"A venom," Golfin went on, "injected by means of a pin or needle. The coroner found—will find, that is—a small puncture in the small of your back on the right side, with some of the venom still imbedded, along with the paste."

"I'll tell you what I'm going to do," I said. "I'm getting out of here." I turned toward the door.

"Wait!" Sarah Fish said. "Mr. Golfin says it will happen when you try to leave."

My momentum left me as my hand touched the doorknob. It flowed out of me. I turned around and faced them.

"Just how do you know all this?" I said, glaring at the little man.

"I suppose I had better tell you," he said. "I'm *Dr.* Golfin."

"Oh," I said.

He reached into his breast pocket and extracted an expensive leather billfold. Looking quite important for his size, he took out a card and extended it to me.

"My specialty is—has been," he said, "amnesiacs. I've made a life study of them."

I looked at the card. It gave the name, Dr. S. L. Golfin, and an address on Wabash, Chicago.

"The phenomenon of amnesia interested me," he went on. "A person suddenly can't remember anything. Perhaps years later memory returns, but there is a gap. Why?"

He smiled at me triumphantly. Sarah Fish nodded sagely.

"Because ..." Golfin lifted his left arm with a flourish and inspected his watch. "One hour and three minutes," he said quietly. Then, "That was the question I asked myself. Why? Unfortunately amnesia is rather rare. The few genuine cases didn't give me enough opportunity to find the answer. I did, however, arrive at several theories about it. And finally I came to the conclusion that amnesia is part of a larger field. I expanded my research to include other phenomena such as prophetic dreams. I was sure I was on the right track, but unfortunately it was impossible to study a person in the process of having a prophetic dream."

"I can see that," I said sympathetically.

"Exactly," Golfin said, blinking up at me. "However, I asked myself, 'Of the several theories, wouldn't the one that also accounts for prophetic dreams be the more probable one?' And of course it's well known that the more a theory explains, the more probable it is of being true."

"Not always," I ventured.

He pondered this, then looked at his watch again. "Fifty-three minutes," he said.

I swallowed.

"But how do amnesia and prophetic dreams tie together?" I asked.

"They are basically the same phenomenon," Golfin said, "with one important difference. In amnesia the conscious mind jumps over a period of time and stays there, going on in normal fashion. In prophetic dreams it does the same, *except that it returns to its starting point.*"

I glanced at Sarah Fish. She was listening intently. It occurred to me that she hadn't heard any of this before either. She was the congenial type. Undoubtedly when Golfin had sprung this murder business on her she hadn't asked questions.

"Now do you see what I'm getting at?" Golfin said. "The mechanism must be the same in both instances. An underlying mechanism. In amnesia a person may suffer a brain injury, or a person may be under a terrific compulsion to escape the present. In either case the person jumps over a period of days or years in, seemingly, an instant—and refuses to return. In prophetic dreams the person jumps into the future to an instant when something crucial is taking place, and returns to the present with memory of it."

I looked at my own watch and said, "Any other time I would like to listen, but what are you driving at?"

He frowned and glanced at his watch. "Forty-one minutes," he said. "This is what I'm driving at. If I could discover the mechanism by which the mind leaps into the future, and returns, I would have a means of doing that myself. I could, possibly, go to tomorrow and buy a newspaper and see what it says, and return to today with that knowledge."

"I see now!" Sarah Fish said, quivering with excitement. "That's how you learned that Mr. Smith is to be murdered!"

"So you did discover a way?" I said.

"I did. That's why I'm here. For some time now I have been going into the future at will, and also into the past. I've learned how to control it, the length of time I stay there, and just how far into the future or the past I go."

"It sounds good," I admitted. "How could you change things?"

He glanced at his watch worriedly. "We haven't much time," he said. "A little over half an hour. What I want to do is this. I have the instruments with me to send you into the future to the moment you are dying. I want you to go there and see if you don't know then who killed you, and how. You will return to the present moment with that knowledge, and be able to avoid death. At least—" He smiled encouragingly. "At least I hope you will."

"And if I don't?"

He shrugged. "This is my first serious attempt to change the past. Sooner or later I will succeed." He had reached into his breast pocket again. Now he brought out something like a fat fountain pen.

"I don't know," I said uneasily. "You sure this doesn't hurt?"

He unscrewed the end of the thing. There was a short hollow needle on it, with what looked like a trigger that had swung out into position against the side.

"I've used it on myself many times," he said. He started toward me.

"Wait a minute," I said, backing up a step and holding up my hand. "This is going to take me up to the instant I'm dying?"

"That's right," he said, "and I want you to try, in that single instant you are there, to find out who did it. Think where you were when it happened, and who might have done it."

"You sure it won't kill me?" I asked.

He took another step toward me. "Of course not," he said.

"Wait a minute," I said, backing up against a bookcase to get away from him. "Why didn't you go farther ahead in time and read in the papers who did it? Wouldn't that have been the best way?"

For a brief instant his eyes flashed with what seemed to me to be madness. I thought of the three-dollar bill. The guy was crazy. It had to be that. He'd been using the stuff on himself. Whatever it was it had affected his mind. He imagined he could send his mind into the future. Or maybe—

I remembered suddenly why I was here. I had followed Golfin in the hopes of getting one of those three-dollar bills. That made it a vicious circle. Sure. It was *he* who was going to murder me, if anyone was. Those other people didn't know me. And he said I was going to be poisoned by venom on a pin or needle—*or was it going to be a hypodermic needle?*

"Don't be afraid, Mr. Smith," Golfin purred. "It's the only hope of saving your life. Your murder was never solved."

"Oh, it is, is it?" I gritted. I snaked out with my hand and wrapped my fingers around the wrist of the hand that held the needle. "Give me that thing," I said.

He struggled. He had a lot of strength for a little man. He pivoted around and tried to pull his wrist free. With his other hand he tried to get hold of the needle. I kept shaking his wrist to keep him from doing it.

Then I remembered his expensive billfold. It probably had the three-dollar bills in it. I simply reached into his breast pocket and appropriated it. He didn't know it was gone.

A second later, with a loud grunt, he twisted violently in a last effort to get free. I heard a sharp snap, and at the same time I felt a sharp pain stab into me.

It was in the small of my back on the right side. *The small of my back on the right side!*

I let go of his wrist. He was just starting to jerk again, and my letting go made him stagger backwards and fall against the bookcase on the far wall. He didn't even know his gadget had gone off!

I did, though. And a strange fatalism was seeping into me, like the emotional effect of a drug. A numbness was beginning to make itself felt along my right side.

Sarah Fish was staring at me, her eyes large and round. Not like a fish though. Too human, too full of concern and sympathy. Maybe she had seen the needle stick me....

Funny ... Golfin came here convinced in his own insane way that he was going to prevent a murder. If he hadn't come, I wouldn't have come either. And if he hadn't come, there wouldn't have been a corpse....

∞

I LOOKED AROUND until I found the door, and headed toward it. My right leg dragged a little as I walked. And I didn't need to go into the future to know what was going to happen. I would make it to the door. Sure. I would open it, and walk through the crowd outside toward the front door. Before I got there I would die. Golfin would never know, maybe, that it was his drug that had killed me. Sarah Fish, convinced by the way it happened that Golfin had been right, would insist to the police that I was okay when I left her.

I could stop right where I was and die in this room. My hand gripped the doorknob and twisted, and the door opened. And I knew I wasn't going to stay in this room. I was going to try to get to the front door.

My whole right side was numb now. I had to walk slowly. Even then I wasn't sure of my next step. And with each step the massive front door seemed farther away.

I wasn't going to make it.

I bumped into someone—or someone bumped into me. I jerked my head around with a snarl starting on my lips. It was George Wile.

"Sorry old boy," he apologized. "I didn't see you."

I blinked at him, an idea forming. Maybe if I could change something—any little thing—I could save myself. What could I change? I didn't know, because I didn't know whether even the change I might make would be part of the future. Still …

"'Sall right, ol' boy," I said, bumping against him. And my hands moved fast. My own wallet went into his pocket, and his went into mine.

I stepped back, grinning. I had at least done something to confuse the issues. I would leave that puzzle behind me. It wouldn't fool anyone though, because they would know who I was. Sarah Fish and Sam Golfin.

My heart was starting to pound painfully. Panic flooded into me. I had to reach that front door. I had to! It was already open, and people were going through it, leaving the party. The distinguished-appearing man was standing there shaking hands with them as they left.

Where was I supposed to drop dead? I wished I had asked Golfin that. I took another step, and another. And, unbelieving, I was at the door.

"Glad you could be here," the distinguished-appearing man said, gripping my hand and letting it go.

He had turned to the next person, and I was standing there, my heart pounding, expecting to drop. Somebody pushed against me gently and said, "Pardon me." I put my hand on the door frame and put one foot over the threshold. I was still standing.

I let go the door frame and put the other foot over the threshold. I was standing on the porch. I sucked in a breath. It was too good to be true. There was a catch to it somewhere. But—

I took another step. Eager haste possessed me. I took quick steps off the porch. I was on the sidewalk. I was still alive!

And somewhere I had lost the numbness in my side.

Around me people were getting in their cars, the doors slamming shut softly. I glanced over my shoulder. More people were coming out of the house.

I waited for no more. Almost running, I went the two blocks to the stop sign and turned toward the drugstore.

"Made it," I said under my voice as I pushed open the door and went in. I slid into the same seat I had occupied before. The same counter girl took my order for coffee. "Black this time," I said. "And where's my paper?"

My heart wasn't pounding any more. I was still shaky, but there wasn't a chance of my dying. Not a chance. I grinned to myself.

My coffee came. Also a paper. I sipped the coffee and tried to get interested in the paper. But I kept going back to what had happened.

Then I heard the sound of police sirens. They approached until they were just outside. I looked out and saw the police cars turn the corner, going in the direction of the house where I had been.

So someone had died after all!

I reached under my coat and touched the spot where the needle had struck me. It was a little sore, but not enough to bother me.

Who had been killed? George Wile? Suddenly I remembered the exchange of wallets I had made. I reached into my hip pocket and took out his wallet.

I looked in the money compartment and saw I had enriched myself by twenty dollars. Grinning, I looked in another pocket of the wallet. There was a package of needles. My grin wiped off. They were ordinary sewing needles. But the pointed ends were covered with what seemed to be gray paint.

The counter girl was at the far end scrubbing the counter. The baldish cashier was on the other side of the store behind a counter, waiting on a man and a woman. I took Golfin's billfold and quickly thumbed through it.

There were several of the three-dollar bills. There were two ones. And there were five twenty-dollar bills. I shoved all the money into my pocket except one of the three-dollar bills.

I made sure no one was looking my way, and dropped Golfin's billfold on the floor, kicking it under the counter behind me in the center aisle where it wouldn't be found unless the janitor swept under there. I decided to do the same with Wile's. After all, if Sam Golfin were right, and there was a murder, I didn't want a couple of strange wallets on me. Nor those coated needles.

I looked at the three-dollar bill in my hand. It was like that other one. Picture of Truman on it, atomic mushroom on the other side, with the atom superimposed. I squinted at the fine print. *Series of 1958.*

That made me frown. Why would someone bother to change the date on phony money? And it was too nice a job of engraving for such a thing too.

I thought of one of the tests for good money. I rubbed the three-dollar bill against the margin of the newspaper. Some of the ink came off.

The wild theory Golfin had fed me was tame compared to what

I was beginning to suspect. I took out the rest of his money and picked out a twenty-dollar bill. Putting the rest back in my pocket, I studied the twenty. I rubbed it against the margin of the newspaper. Ink came off. It was genuine money.

Taking a deep breath, I squinted at the fine print. *Series of 1964.*

I looked at the rest of the money I had taken from Golfin. The two ones were okay. All the rest had dates in the future. I knew money. I could spot a phony bill a block away. It was real money.

Either a master counterfeiter had—Another thought struck me. I compared the serial numbers of the bills. All different. That clinched it. They weren't phony.

That meant that Golfin was *actually from the future himself.* Then why had he given me and Sarah Fish that story about prophetic dreams and amnesia? I thought about that a bit and nodded to myself. He wanted to give us something we could believe. We wouldn't have believed a raw statement that he was from the future. Those three-dollar bills …

The more I thought about them the less they seemed like a gag. I tried to recall every detail of Golfin's passing it when he bought his cigarettes. He hadn't done it like he was pulling a gag. He had taken his change and walked out. He didn't know he had done anything wrong. He had assumed a three-dollar bill was used here—or now, rather.

My coffee was cold. The girl was looking at me as if she wanted to close up. I smiled at her and tossed a quarter on the counter and went out on the sidewalk.

I debated what to do. Should I forget the whole thing? Or should I take a walk back to Sarah Fish's house and see what was going on? I decided on the latter.

∞

HER HOUSE WAS DARK. No police cars were there. That was not what I had expected. With a murder, there should be police cars, and the place should be lit up. Or maybe not. It had been an hour since I left the place.

I went back to the drugstore and caught the bus down to the Davis Street El station. Riding on the elevated it occurred to me that maybe I'd better not go to my apartment. If the police had gotten my wallet from George Wile they might be waiting for me.

I decided to rent a room for the night and wait until morning. Then I changed my mind. If I went back to my room I could claim Wile had picked my pocket. If the police were looking for me they would eventually get me anyway, since I already had a record of three arrests for this and that.

I sighed and relaxed, and after a while the train dipped down into the subway, and I got off and had a late snack at the corner cafeteria.

∞

IT WAS ALMOST MIDNIGHT when I climbed the stairs to my apartment. When I opened the door the phone was ringing. I turned on the light and closed the door, and answered it.

"Ben Smith?" a strange voice said. "This is George Wile."

"Oh," I said. I did some quick thinking. "Oh!" I said in a different tone. "I remember you. How'd you know my number. Did you find my wallet? That must be it. I lost it. Thanks a lot for calling me about it. I'll meet you tomorrow and get it back."

"It was in my pocket," he said coldly. "And my own was missing. I want it back."

"Yours was missing?" I said. "Hey, wait a minute. If you think I got it you're crazy. Somebody played a trick on us. There must have been a pickpocket at Sarah Fish's tonight."

"There was," he said coldly. "You. I took the trouble of calling the police and found out. I want my wallet and I want it tonight."

"I don't have it. No kidding." I said worriedly. "I'm handing you the straight goods. By the way, what happened after I left? I heard the police sirens."

"Someone had called them and said there was a murder. They were pretty sore about it."

"And there wasn't? Ha Ha?" I said.

"Quit stalling, Smith," Wile said. "I want my wallet back. And everything in it."

"Haven't got it," I said.

A long sigh came over the phone. "All right," Wile said. "I sort of expected this. I'll give you five hundred dollars for it."

I took the phone from my face and stared at it, thinking. Talking sounds came from the receiver. I put it back to my ear and said, "Come again? I didn't hear you."

"You heard me all right," Wile said. "Okay, I can get you two thousand dollars from the bank tomorrow. Meet me at eleven o'clock at State and Washington, northeast corner."

"Okay," I said. "Be sure and bring me *my* wallet."

"I will," he said smoothly. His tone became worried. "Is my wallet in a *safe* place?"

"Sure," I said, thinking of the spot under the counter where I had slid it with my foot. "You don't need to worry about it at all."

The line was dead. I realized suddenly that he had trapped me into an admission that I had his wallet.

This wasn't the same as a little light-finger work on a crowded train, or getting a rubber check chased, or any of the many things I did when the opportunity arose, to pay my rent. Wile didn't just want these poison needles back. He was planning to kill me to keep me quiet. But he wanted the needles and his wallet back too. First.

I thought of Golfin and his reading in the papers that I had been murdered, and it wasn't funny. I locked the door and wedged a chair under the knob. Wile now knew for sure I was the one who had his wallet. He could be on his way down to kill me right now.

I started packing.

It wasn't until I was almost packed that I suddenly became aware of someone standing behind me. I jerked around in alarm. It was Sam Golfin.

"How'd you get in here?" I blurted out.

"I've been waiting here ever since tomorrow," he said. "I had to see you."

I grinned at him thinly. "I didn't get murdered at Sarah's after all," I remarked dryly.

"No, thank God," Golfin said. "It proves that the past can be changed. I'd hoped it could." He frowned. "But unfortunately in preventing your murder at Sarah's a new future came into existence. I have to do it all over again."

"What do you mean?" I asked.

"Tomorrow when I came to see you, you were in here—dead. The door was unlocked. That's how I got in."

"Oh fine!" I snorted. "See what I'm doing? I'm packing. In another five minutes I'll be on my way to parts unknown."

"I only wish that were true," Golfin said sadly.

"Look," I said. "I wish you'd get out and leave me alone. You want to know why I almost got killed last night?"

"Yes, I do," Golfin said. "That's something the police couldn't find out—in that other future, I mean."

"I'll tell you," I said. "I didn't know anything about Sarah Fish's place. I probably would never have gone there except for you. You bought a pack of cigarettes in the drugstore. Remember?"

Golfin blinked his eyes, then nodded.

"You paid for them with a three-dollar bill."

"What is wrong with that?" Golfin asked.

"Nothing," I said slowly, "except that there aren't any three-dollar bills."

"Oh dear me," Golfin said. "Of course there aren't. It completely slipped my mind!"

"I wanted one of those three-dollar bills," I said. "The druggist wouldn't let me have the one you left, so I went to Sarah Fish's place to find you and get one."

A knock sounded at the door.

"It's the man who's going to kill you," Sam said.

"And there isn't any other way out of here," I said. "How are you going to get me out of this one?"

"I don't know," he mused. He looked from me to the door, his eyes thoughtful. "I'm beginning to see something," he said. "It's very interesting. So you went to the Fish residence because of me. Hmmm. I wonder…. It doesn't seem possible, but …."

"What doesn't seem possible?" I asked.

He smiled apologetically. "There really isn't anything that can be done about that man in the hall." The knocking was repeated, more loudly. "And this future is quite hopeless for you…."

Whoever was in the hall was trying some kind of key in the lock.

"If I owned a gun it wouldn't be," I said, watching the door bend in under pressure from outside.

"If you only knew who it was!" Golfin groaned.

"But I do!" I said.

"You said at Sarah's that you didn't," Golfin snapped.

"I didn't, then," I said. Quickly I told him about George Wile and the package of poisoned needles. "He's obviously planning on murdering someone. Maybe at Sarah's last night," I concluded hastily, my eye on the door. "My switching wallets with him stopped that. Now he's got to kill me before he can go ahead with this other murder, or I could put the finger on him."

"Why—didn't—you—say—so—before?" Golfin said, glaring at me with annoyance.

The door splintered a little, the noise sounding like a shot. I took my eyes off Golfin to look, and when I looked back Golfin was darting at me, his hypodermic gadget in his hand and what looked like murder in his eye.

I tried to grab his wrist. This time he was too fast for me. He evaded my clutch and was behind me before I could turn. I felt a sharp pain stab at the base of my skull. I started to turn. The room blurred as a wave of dizziness swept over me….

∞

"HERE'S YOUR COFFEE, sir."

I looked at the girl behind the counter, then down at my newspaper. "Thanks," I said. My stomach felt funny. I felt just like a guy I knew once who had a premonition he was going to die. Heartburn, I decided hastily. But I felt nervous.

I took a sip of the hot coffee and tried to concentrate on the paper. Then I became aware of the little man. I felt instantly I had seen him someplace before, but I couldn't place him.

"A package of Camels," he said to the cashier.

"That will be twenty cents," the baldish cashier said.

The little man handed him a bill he had been holding in his hand. "By the way," he said smoothly as the cashier glanced at it, "could you tell me the way to Sarah Fish's residence?"

The little man glanced at me out of the corner of his eye. He seemed to know me, but gave no sign of recognition. The cashier was giving him directions. I was listening, but I was trying to puzzle out the strange feeling that I had been through all this before. And it wasn't until the little man had left that it seeped into my consciousness that something was queer about that bill.

"Hey!" I said to the cashier. "What kind of bill did that little guy give you?"

"Why, a—a—Oh good Lord."

We examined it together. It was a three-dollar bill. And instead of surprise, I felt the jaws of a trap closing in on me. I listened to the cashier babble about playing gags on his friends with it. A part of me wanted to turn my back on the whole thing and forget it.

But some force pulled me in the direction the little man had gone. As I walked I relaxed. I shrugged off the strange feeling I had. I told myself I didn't believe in premonitions.

A PARTY OF SOME SORT was in full swing at the Sarah Fish place. I nodded to myself. I could go in and mix with the crowd. I could pick this little man's pocket. Maybe a few more. The worst that could happen would be that they wouldn't let me in.

Beside the huge door was a button. I pressed it and heard a series of chimes ring out. A few seconds later the door swung open and a middle aged man with a jovial expression said, "Come in, come in. I'm George Wile. Sarah's somewhere. What's your name? Sorry I can't keep track of all Sarah's friends."

"Ben Smith," I said, stepping inside.

"Sarah'll show up in a minute," George Wile said, and promptly forgot me. That was okay by me. I had taken an instant dislike to him.

I stood near the door looking around, trying to spot the little man. A gorgeous young thing held a tray in front of my face until I took a tall glass that contained, I discovered, an excellent Tom Collins.

Suddenly I saw the little man. He was at the edge of the group surrounding a distinguished appearing man who was talking. I edged over near the crowd and sized things up. It would be a cinch.

I crowded against the little man, then jerked as though someone had shoved me. At the same time my free hand snaked in and got his wallet.

"Sorry," I murmured. "Someone pushed me."

The little man looked up at me and smiled. And I had a strange feeling that he had been expecting it. I could have sworn he even knew I had his wallet, and was laughing at me.

There was one obvious answer. He was a cop and he knew me. He'd take his time and get me with the goods. He didn't look like a cop but—

I looked for him and he had disappeared.

I tried to locate him, meanwhile sipping my Collins as though I belonged here. Then I did something I always do unconsciously as a matter of habit. I felt in my hip pocket to make sure my own wallet hadn't been stolen by some other pickpocket. It was gone!

So that was it! The little man was a pickpocket. I thought I had seen him someplace before! I grinned suddenly, wondering if he had really missed his billfold yet.

I kept looking for him. Then things happened fast. I saw the little man sliding away from the man who had let me into the house. George Wile. I took a step after the little man. My eyes jerked back to George when he uttered a scream and clutched at his back. He fell forward, his arms and legs jerking.

I pulled my eyes away, searching for the little man. A crowd was rushing around George Wile. I heard someone—a woman—scream, "My God! He's dead!"

I saw the little man at the front door. He slipped out as I pushed through the crowd toward him. I went as fast as I dared. When I reached the sidewalk I saw him running toward the drugstore.

I ran after him, gaining rapidly. He looked over his shoulder and saw me. Then—

He just vanished. Right in front of my eyes. He couldn't have darted off the walk into the bushes.

I stopped, not believing my eyes, and started searching the lawns carefully. A couple of minutes later I heard sirens coming toward this part of town.

I hid between two houses and watched the police cars pull up in front of Sarah Fish's place. Then I went to the bus line.

∞

A FEW HOURS LATER, after a lot of riding around town I climbed up to the sidewalk from the subway. A night extra was being shouted.

"Big murdah in Evanston!"

And I knew before I read the paper that it would give my name as the murdered man. Premonition. I was beginning to believe in it now.

I went to an all-night café and ordered a hamburger plate and read the paper. They had identified the victim by the wallet they found on him. My wallet, of course. And that meant that the little man had planted it on him and then killed him. With a poisoned needle the papers said.

Why?

I gave up trying to figure it out after a while and went to my apartment. I had made up my mind to get out of town. They might find out the victim's real identity, and then they would come looking for me to find out why my wallet was on him.

I locked the door and began packing clothes into a suitcase. I became aware after a while of someone standing behind me.

I jerked around in alarm. It was the little man.

"You!" I blurted. "How'd you get in here?" I doubled a fist and started toward him. He had killed a man and planted my wallet on the corpse.

Then, suddenly, a queer distortion blanketed my mind. I had a strange conviction that things were happening just the way they had happened before—many times before—only not at different times, but this very instant.

Abruptly, like a veil drawing away from a window, the distortion vanished. With preternatural clarity everything that had happened flooded into memory.

"Good!" Golfin said. "I see the time-lines have emerged as true memories. And this time I saved your life."

"You think so?" I snarled. "The police will be after me by morning. They'll pin the murder on me—the murder you committed."

He was shaking his head. "I didn't kill George Wile. Let me explain what happened. But go on with your packing. I can talk while you work."

I nodded.

"In the first time-line," Golfin said, "the one I started out to investigate, you were actually killed. I know now how it happened. You see, Sarah Fish is a blackmailer. George Wile was one of her victims. To get out of her clutches he had planned on killing her. It was a perfect setup for him. Several of her blackmail victims were there. All he had to do was stick her with the poisoned needle and sit back. Nothing could be pinned on him. Motive? A dozen of those present had equal motives.

"But you were there. A pickpocket. You lifted his wallet. He wouldn't have felt your light touch ordinarily, but he was acutely conscious of those spare poisoned needles. He had one in his fingers. Within a few moments Sarah would have been killed. You changed things. He killed you instead, and in the excitement stole back his wallet. And of course he didn't go through with his original plan to kill Sarah Fish. And also of course, the police never solved your murder. That's why I chose it in my first attempt to change the past. It was an ideal mystery. I could solve it and at the same time save your life.

"I went into the past and watched your every move. But George Wile was too smart. Even watching I couldn't find out who had done it. So I went back into the past again and began my great experiment, *an attempt to alter what has already happened.*

"I succeeded—but not the way I had hoped. There is an inertia to events. That inertia in events made you steal his wallet the second time—and plant your own on him. You left before he discovered the switch. He came after you to kill you here. It was then you gave me the identity of your killer. After that I went back to my original point again. At the proper time I did what you had done. I picked George Wile's pocket. He felt me do it. Again—the inertia of events—he tried to stick me with the poisoned needle. But I was ready for him. I deflected his hand and shoved. He stuck himself."

Golfin grinned. "Sure I planted your wallet on him. But who can say whether it was my own free will or the inertia of events that made me do it? The morning papers will carry the story exactly the same as it was in the first time-line. A tremendous inertia of a single event."

"But what about me?" I said wildly. "The police will check. They'll know he isn't me."

Golfin shrugged. "I doubt it," he said. "My guess is that Sarah will identify him as you and keep quiet. To protect her racket, George will be buried as Ben Smith. George Wile's relatives will report him missing. He'll never be found. 'Your' murder will remain unsolved."

"I'm getting out anyway," I said. "I don't want to chance it."

"Then why not come with me?" Golfin said. "Now that I know I can change the past I'm going to start doing it in earnest."

"Go with you?" I said.

"You could work for me," Golfin said persuasively. "I would pay you far more than you average picking pockets, and it would be far more exciting work."

"Say …" I said thoughtfully. "That's not a bad idea. I guess I owe you something, too, for saving my life." I nodded. "Okay. But where do we go?"

"Not where," Sam Golfin said. "To when. We're going to my present—a future year not too far removed from 1954."

He took out his hypodermic gadget and came toward me. I retreated a step, then stood still, the palms of my hands suddenly wet with perspiration.

"Good boy," he said. "It won't hurt much."

∞

I WENT INTO THE DRUGSTORE and up to the cigar counter. "A pack of Camels," I said to the cashier. I took out a three-dollar bill and handed it to him as he slid the pack toward me.

"Fifty cents out of three dollars," he said absently.

I nodded, thinking of the first time I had seen a three-dollar bill.

That was a long time ago, as time goes. Back in fifty-four. I was a pickpocket then, in case you want to know. Now—I'm working for Sam Golfin.

Investigations. Any place, any Time.

Time Out for Redheads

Miriam Allen deFord

Originally published in *Startling Stories*, Summer 1955

IS NAME WAS Mikel Skot. He was thirty-four, five-feet-ten and lean, with decent features and all his hair and quite nice brown eyes. But somehow he always seemed to give the impression of being of indeterminate age, and slightly dusty. He lived alone, he gravitated between his job and his lodgings, and since the age of fourteen he had never known a girl well enough to call her by her first name.

For twelve years, ever since 2827, he had sold tickets at one of the windows of Time Travel Tours, Unlimited. If raises hadn't been automatic, he would never have had one, though he was punctual, faithful, honest, quick and accurate. Even the other ticket-sellers still called him Citizen Skot.

He had never budged from his cozy era—even though, as an employee, he was entitled to take any tour he wished, on his semi-annual vacation, at no cost to him beyond the planetary sales tax— nor had he ever left his native city, let alone his native planet. He was too shy even to realize he was lonely.

This morning there was the usual rush. Staggered vacations meant that any time of the year was the busy season for TTT. Skillfully Mikel Skot arranged tours and calculated rates.

"Two weeks in Rome, 45 BC? That will be creds 850, Citizen. You get your costume and equipment in Room 104, right off the Teleport. Yes, I'm sure they'll have a Latin language-transformer you can hire." "England in 1600, one month, reservation in the name of Chas Rusl. Yes, I have it right here. That will be creds 500, please." "You mean you want a ticket for here in Los, for a week six years ago in February? Why, yes, it's a little unusual, but—oh, certainly, I understand—a second honeymoon. Congrats, Citizen—not many couples stay together that long! Just a min, while I look up the rate for two."

The queue seemed endless, and crowds of travelers who already had their tickets were pushing their way through the doors in back of the ticket-office to the Teleport itself, together with the friends who were seeing them off. If Mikel had had a moment to spare, which he hadn't, he might have wondered, as so often before, at the numbers of people everybody except himself seemed to know.

The morning wore on, and he was beginning to think longingly of 13:30 o'clock, when his lunchtime relief would arrive and he could sit in a quiet corner of an Autocaf and watch the tridimens screen for the day's news while he ate his favorite vitatabs and smoked a healthcig.

Then everything happened all at once.

The girl standing at his ticket-window was a redhead. Her eyes were green, with little dancing amber lights in them, and she smiled at him as if he were the kind of man girls do smile at, and not ineffectual Mikel Skot.

"Can you tell me," she began, in a warm, slightly husky voice.

Then she screamed loudly and collapsed.

THERE WERE SHOUTS and jostling and milling around, and somebody leaned over the counter and abruptly thrust something into his hand. He stood there dazed, grabbing the object, whatever it was. Then he leaned over the counter. The girl was lying there, very still. On one side of her a pool of blood was slowly forming on the floor.

The guards were coming from all directions, trying to get some kind of quiet and order into the excited throng. Mikel looked down at the thing in his hand.

It was a knife, a steel knife with a wooden handle. It was obviously an antique, and of great value. And it was smeared with fresh blood.

Mikel Skot lost his head entirely. Never before had he, or anyone he had ever heard of, been involved even remotely in any kind of violence. He never even took in historical crime plays. The redheaded girl was dead, and he held in his hand the knife that had killed her. And she had been the first girl who had smiled at him for years.

He wanted out—now!

He reached behind him and grabbed a ticket at random, not even looking to see what date it was. He punched it hastily for a week. Nobody was looking at him; everybody was still yelling at everybody else, and the sweating guards were trying to line people up and blocking the doors so that they could not get away. Mikel ran to the corridor back of the counters, which the ticket-sellers used, and saw that the company door to the Teleport was open. Out there, what with parties singing "Happy Timetrav to You," or noisily greeting homecomers, and the loudspeaker directing passengers to their proper stations, and the roar of the take-offs and returnjets, nobody seemed to have noticed that anything was wrong in the ticket-office.

MIKEL GLANCED AROUND ONCE to be sure that nobody was watching him, and slipped through the door. He was still holding the knife. Automatically he thrust it into his belt-pouch.

It was typical of him that after twelve years not one of the Teleport attendants knew him by sight. He thrust his ticket at the nearest one. The man glanced at it (three other travelers were trying to get his attention at the same time) and said "Platform Eight." Mikel hurried there.

Before he reached it he remembered something. He had punched the ticket for duration, but not for place. Well, that was all right. If it had no place-punch, it would mean Los itself. He was escaping into his own city.

The attendant at Eight took his ticket, then peered at him dubiously. "You haven't clothes for the period, Citizen. Go to Room 104 and—"

"It doesn't matter," Mikel interrupted him. He was in a fever to be gone. "I'm—it's a research project," he added in a sudden inspiration which didn't make sense even to himself, but which the attendant, used to strange statements from travelers, accepted without comment. He sealed the timeporter on to Mikel's wrist, set it for return in a week, and helped him into the telechamber.

There was a swift moment when his head felt empty and his stomach heaved: and Mikel Skot found himself sitting on an iron bench in a park.

He had a week now to think things over. He was in Los—he had to be, his ticket said so.

But when?

He looked about him. It must be the middle of the day, the same time it had been before, and the park was full of people on their lunch-hour. They were dressed weirdly—the men and half the women wore tight cylindrical garments, one on each leg. The upper part of their bodies were covered with various kinds of brightly-colored cloth, though occasionally he saw a woman who wore only a breast-holder above her bare midriff! Mikel, in his belted tunic, huddled in a corner of his bench, fearful of notice. But nobody paid any attention to him, and once a man passed who had on a tunic too—a long white one, over bare feet and under long hair and a flowing beard. Apparently in this period people dressed as they pleased—at least in Los.

The city itself, what part of it he could see from his vantage-point, was stranger than the people. There were no moving sidewalks, and no weather-canopies over the streets—though perhaps these had only been removed for the dry season. The buildings looked shrunken and tiny—hardly one seemed to be more than thirty or forty stories high. Archaic buses and motor-cars, apparently powered by some non-atomic fuel, plied the actual streets, instead of being confined to subways. The skies were almost empty of planes, and those he saw were incredibly clumsy and slow. There was obviously no freeway for helicopters.

IT WAS SELF-EVIDENT that he was in some year of the remote past, though just which, he had no idea. He wished he had taken time to glance at the ticket before he handed it in. He wished he had studied history komikbooks, or given more than a cursory glance at the telescreen propinforms of TTT. There was something to be said, after all, for the General Educationalists, cranks as they were.

Certainly this was not his Los—his giant city stretching from Mex to Sanfran without a break. This was a little place of probably not much more than two million inhabitants. Well, here he was for a week, and he'd better find out how he was going to eat and sleep. Properly equipped time travelers had money of the right period, but the cred checks in his pouch would do him no good now. What did he have on him that could be exchanged for board and lodging?

Only one object of undoubted value. The knife.

Surreptitiously and with distaste he took it out and looked at it. The blood had dried on it and doubtless left traces on the lining of his pouch. It was probably covered with the fingerprints of the murderer as well as with his own. But it was all he had.

In the middle of the park there was a fountain, with a pool around it. Casually Mikel Skot strolled over to it and sat down on the ledge. When he was sure nobody was looking he dipped the knife in the water and scrubbed it dry on the inner hem of his tunic. There would still be traces of blood which any chemist could find, of course; but nobody here would be examining it for that. Since anyone could see that it was of immense value, he would have to account for possession of it. He could say it was an heirloom.

Putting it back in his pouch he approached a fat man on a bench nearby.

"Where is the nearest history museum, please, Citizen?" he asked politely.

The man looked up. He had been scanning a large piece of paper which Mikel, with a thrill, recognized from one of his few visits to the Museum of Antiquities. It was a thing called a newspaper, which had antedated the tridimens telescreen. He remembered that the specimens he had seen had borne dates at the top, and if he could read the archaic printing he could find out what year it was. But the man folded it up and thrust it under his arms as he answered.

"History museum?" he echoed. "Gosh, bud, I don't know. I'm a stranger here myself—just got in from Kansas yesterday. You a foreigner?" he asked with frank curiosity. "You got a funny accent. And you sure look funny."

A foreigner—that was a good one! But Mikel had no time to waste. He murmured "Excuse," and left. The man stared after him and made a gesture which Mikel did not understand—describing a circle in the air near his forehead.

Mikel walked to the edge of the little park and looked about him. Across the street was a store with newspapers in racks in front of it. He could go over there and see the dates. But what did it really matter? With his ignorance of all but the haziest generalities of history—he thought that once, thousands of years ago, Los had belonged to the Spaniards, and after that there was some kind of war that was maybe called the American Revolution or the Civil War or the World War, he was not sure which—it wouldn't do him much good to know whether he was in, say, 1820 or 1960 or 2080. Besides, he was afraid to cross that street full of clumsy vehicles, and with neither an overpass nor an underpass. Nowhere could he see anything that resembled a museum.

FARTHER DOWN on the same side of the street on which he stood, he saw something that looked faintly promising. He walked down to it, and found a window full of odd-looking primitive objects, the nature of some of which he could not guess. But there were knives among them, and a sign said, in ancient spelling, "Jewelry Bought and Sold." On an impulse he walked in.

A man in another queer garment—some kind of cloth upper, with a white linen thing beneath it and a ribbon tied around his neck—looked up without surprise at Mikel's literally untimely garb, and said: "Yes, sir?"

Mikel drew out the knife.

"Very valuable," he said. "An heirloom. How much will you give me?"

The man shrank back, not as if he were afraid of the knife, but as if he were suddenly afraid of Mikel.

"You kidding me?" he asked. "Or is this a stick-up?"

Mikel was not sure what the words meant, so he merely shook his head.

"Then are you nuts? There's nothing valuable about that thing. It's just an ordinary kitchen knife."

"Not valuable?" Mikel's face fell. "But look—wooden handle, steel blade."

"So what? Every knife has a wooden handle and a steel blade."

"You will not give me money for it?"

"Of course not. We don't buy junk."

There was no use arguing. One age's antique is another age's junk. Mikel sighed and departed quietly. How was he to get food and shelter for a week?

He went back to the park and sat down again on a bench. He put the knife back in his pouch.

This was what came of panicking for the first time in his humdrum life. A sudden image of the redheaded girl came before his mind—her green eyes and her smile. That girl—she was so pretty—and she had smiled at him, whom girls never noticed. And then she had been killed. Now that it was too late, he wished he had stayed, whatever might have happened to him. He wanted to help, to avenge her; he wanted to be home again.

His stomach reminded him sharply that he had had no lunch. He had never heard how long a man could go without eating. Could he even live through the week?

He sat there disconsolately, his eyes fixed on the ground. On his wrist was sealed the little gadget that was his only means of ever seeing 2839 again.

SOMEBODY CAME AND SAT DOWN beside him. Deep in thought, he did not even glance up. A voice said, "Can you tell me what time it is? My watch is broken and there's no clock around here."

"Watch"—that meant "to be alert." "Clock"—that was an ancient time-measuring device, he thought. The only way Mikel knew to tell the time was to glance at the ceiling of any room, or if he were outdoors to tune in on his miniature tridimens gadget, attached to his belt. He dialed it now, but there was no response. Of course not—it wouldn't work across perhaps a thousand years.

"I'm sorry," he answered. "I can't."

He turned as he spoke. He jumped violently.

The speaker was a girl. She had red hair and green eyes. Otherwise there was no resemblance, though she too was pretty. But red hair and green eyes seemed to be haunting him.

"What's that thing on your left wrist, then?" asked the girl spunkily.

Mikel reddened. Rule Five of the booklets he handed out with the tickets to all travelers leaped into his mind: "Remember, you cannot change the course of history. To avoid confusion and difficulty, avoid revealing to any person you meet in other time-periods the true nature of your presence there."

He broke the rule, and was sorry at once.

"It's a timeporter," he said, "set for my return home."

The girl laughed. "That's a good one. I thought I'd heard everything since I came to this crazy place. What are you, an Arab, dressed in that tablecloth?"

"I was born right here in Los," Mikel announced with dignity. "I've always lived here."

"So they grow them crazy here right from the start! Then where's your home you're 'set' to return to?"

"Here in Los."

The girl stood up hastily, a look of alarm on her face.

"Oh, please," Mikel cried, "don't go. I can explain. Perhaps you can help me."

She sat down again dubiously.

"Well, I'm a sucker for a good story," she said. "Shoot."

"I—I wouldn't shoot. I have no weapon."

That wasn't true—he did have a weapon: the knife. But he could hardly mention that. Anyway, the girl only laughed again.

"Wisecracks, yet," she said unintelligibly. "Well, what's the story?"

"I am from this place, but I am not from your time," Mikel began laboriously; he was utterly unaccustomed to social conversation with a woman. "I am from—with me it is 2839."

"What in the—look, what are you advertising? Some science fiction magazine?"

"I don't understand that word—adver—what is it? Please believe me. I shouldn't tell you, I'm breaking a rule. But it is true."

"Go on." She fixed him with a skeptical glance.

"I was—I am a ticket-seller for Time Travel Tours. This morning—I mean what was to me this morning—a customer was killed at my window."

He plunged ahead. She listened in silence, a peculiar expression in her eyes.

"So you see," he concluded, "I am here for a week. But then I go back—the timeporter will see to that. I *want* to go—I'm sorry I ran away. But I'm sure the police will say I did it, because of the knife."

"Let's see it."

He brought it out.

"Why, that's just an ordinary kitchen carving knife," she said, just as the man in the store had done. "I suppose you would call it an antique in—what was it?—2839. I still say you're haywire—or else this is some new racket I don't get."

"I don't understand."

"Okay, I guess you wouldn't—in 2839. The language would change plenty in 886 years." Once more her laugh rang out. "I'll say you keep it up fine—that funny half-foreign way you pronounce your words. But I'll play along, and pretend this is all on the up-and-up. Even so, it's haywire—crazy. Because the dumbest cop in the world wouldn't suspect you of the murder. Anybody'd know the murderer just got rid of the knife the quickest way he could. Gosh, you were behind your window, weren't you, and she was in front of it? Where was her stab wound?"

"Wait—it's hard for me to understand. 'Cop'—is that slang for police? And the blood"—he shuddered—"came from her side. Either someone in front or someone behind her could have done it."

"But they'll find out right away, won't they, that you didn't know the girl? They'll find out who she was, and they'll grill everybody she knew, to see who had a reason for wanting her out of the way.... Listen to me! I'm as big a nut as you are. I'm talking just as if the whole thing really happened."

"It did happen," Mikel assured her earnestly. "No, I didn't know her. I don't know any girls at all. I'm—I'm not attractive to women."

"Why, you're not so bad," said the girl kindly. "I think you're kind of cute—or would be, if you weren't rigged up in those outlandish clothes," she paused, then continued, "Well, if you can prove you didn't know her, what have you got to worry about?"

"The knife. And that I lost my head and ran."

The girl nodded. "Leave the knife here, then. Or would that change the course of history?" She smiled. "Of course, what you ought to have done was hand it right over. Then if it was such a great antique they'd not only have the guy's fingerprints but they'd also find out who knew her that worked in a museum or had a chance to steal it from one. That's elementary homicide procedure."

"You see," said Mikel, "this also you won't believe. But our police are not conditioned to take care of killings. This is the first time in my whole life that I have ever even heard of one, except by accident. The psychologists wouldn't allow anyone to grow up who had murderous tendencies that couldn't be sublimated."

"They let that one slip by them, didn't they? And do you mean that in the great scientific future they tell us about, the police won't know as much about handling a homicide case as any hick constable knows today? Who're you trying to kid?"

"We do not have crime. The police are to guard traffic and to take up for reconditioning anybody who doesn't obey the civil rules. I don't know much history, but I know there once were wars, and then there were experts in war. Now—in my time—we have no wars, so there are no experts. In the same way we have no experts in crime."

"Then what would they do to you, if they did convict you of this murder you didn't commit?"

"I don't know. There is no penalty for murder because there have been no murders for so long. This will be a world affair; the police will refer it to the Supreme Council, and they will decide what to do. I suppose they will have me euthanized as an atavistic deviant. That's why I lost my head. It was a totally new experience and I haven't been conditioned to new experiences. But even if they don't convict me, they'll punish me for running away. They'll demote me, perhaps all the way back to where I started twelve years ago."

"It doesn't sound like much of a brave new world to me," said the girl in a disparaging tone. "What's your name—or do you just have numbers?"

"My name is Mikel Skot."

"Michael Scott—well, that sounds like a regular name, anyway. Mine's Betty French, by the way."

"Many grats to you, Citizen French. You have given me good advice. I know now it is my duty to take the knife back with me, and give it to the police. I shall tell them also about looking for somebody in a museum, as you suggested. But there will be no fingerprints—I washed the knife in that fountain, when I hoped to sell it. I forgot it must exist in my era, or the murder could not have occurred.

"But that is not my big problem now. I have no money of your time. How shall I live until I can go home?"

Betty French seemed to stiffen. She looked at him disgustedly. "I get it now," she said. "I might have known. This is just a new way of panhandling. I certainly admire it—it's a work of art. Well, I got my money's worth. I'll pay for it."

She opened her handbag, drew out a dollar bill, and laid it on Mikel's knee. He gazed at it curiously, but made no attempt to pick it up.

"Is that your kind of money?" he asked. "What do I do in exchange for it?"

"Oh, let's drop it," she sighed wearily. "My lunch-hour's up, anyway. Take it—it'll buy you a hamburger and coffee, and then you can tell your tale to the next comer and maybe get enough for a bed in a flophouse. Brother, you must have told it plenty, to get it all down so pat. It's a wonder I've missed you before—or are you just starting to work this neighborhood?"

She snapped her bag shut and stood up.

"Please—I don't understand—why are you so angry?"

At the desperation in his voice she turned and stopped.

"Look—I really have to get back to the office. This is an act, isn't it? Come clean—aren't you panhandling?"

"What does 'panhandling' mean?"

"Oh, I give up! I guess you're just looney, after all. All right, Mike, let's call it a day. You keep that buck, and now you just go to the nearest police station and tell them your story. They'll take you over to the psychiatric ward of the county hospital and you can get free board and lodging there."

Mikel turned pale and shivered.

"Oh, no," he breathed. "I'm not insane. If you don't believe me, no one else will. And the hospital will euthanize me."

"Is that what they do to crazy people in—in your time?"

"Of course. And they punish the psychologist who didn't detect the tendency and have the person euthanized in childhood."

"Suppose I give you my word they won't do that to you here and now? They'll just observe you for a few days and then they'll have you committed to a state hospital."

"You are quite positive? If I can be sure of being alive a week from now, no matter where I am, when the timeporter checks I'll go back home."

"Even if you're in a padded cell?"

"It won't matter where."

"Well, then, your problem's solved, isn't it? I'll show you how to get to the station."

"I must eat first. I'm very hungry. And what were those things you said if I should get—hamburger and coffee? They are—original foods? Our food is all synthetic."

"You don't have to keep this up with me any more. There's a quick lunch place." She pointed.

"And they won't mind in this Autocaf that I'm not dressed like the others?"

"In this burg? They wouldn't notice if you wandered around in a loincloth. Now I've got to go. This is the wackiest thing that ever happened to me, whatever it really means. Well, good luck, Mike!"

"Grats to you, Citizen French, from deep in my pineal. Oh, wait just one min more please!"

"What is it now?"

"You have given me so much to tell our police. But won't they wonder why this man killed the girl?"

"They can ask him when they catch them, can't they? But it's perfectly obvious. She was buying a ticket, wasn't she?"

"Yes, certainly."

"Well, that meant she was going away—leaving him, doesn't it? So he was in love with her—maybe she was his wife—and he couldn't take it. Maybe she was going to some other guy—how do I know? He found out she was deserting him, so he got hold of the knife, and followed her."

"But I don't see why." Mikel was utterly bewildered. "She was a free agent, like anybody else. He couldn't object to her leaving if she no longer loved him—he didn't own her. That doesn't make sense. If I tell one of our police *that* theory, she will surely think I'm insane."

"She?"

"All our police are women, of course. Women are naturally gifted at keeping order."

"You tell that to our cops, and they'll surely get you tucked away in a nice hospital, but fast. Well, why else *would* he kill her?"

"I don't know. That's why I asked you—you know so much more about such things, in your barb—in your time."

"Your policewoman will have to figure it out for herself. So long, Mike." She shook her head, smiling. "Will I have a tale to tell the crowd—if they don't decide I've gone nuts myself! Good-by!"

"Goobie, Citizen, and grats again."

Still smiling, she hurried down the path out of the park.

WHEN HE COULD SEE HER no longer, Mikel stood up and began hesitantly to walk toward the restaurant she had pointed out. Fortunately, it was on the same side of the street, not far past the shop where he tried to sell the knife.

This was not going to be plez, not at all plez. Despite what this Beti French had told him, he was nervous about putting himself in the hands of either the police or psychologist of this barbarous era. But there didn't seem to be anything else he could do. His conversation with the redheaded girl had shown him clearly what kind of reception he would meet from anyone else he ventured to approach.

First he must eat—he was ravenous. He dared not ask for any food except the two things the girl had mentioned, whatever they were like. Presumably the money she had given him would be enough.

The restaurant had a long counter of some white substance, with stools fixed before it. Only one man sat there eating, but behind it stood another man dressed in white, with a white cap on his head. Mikel perched himself on the nearest stool.

"Hamburger, coffee, please," he said, and laid Beti's money beside him on the counter.

The other customer looked up and eyed him sharply, but the man behind the counter merely yelled "One on a bun!" through a hole in the wall. "Mustard?" he asked, "Onions? Cream?"

"No, Citizen. Hamburger, coffee," Mikel repeated, flustered.

"A joker!" the man grunted. "This town! You in the movies, bud?"

Mikel stared.

"He wants a burger without and coffee with," the other customer put in suddenly. He picked up his dishes and slid down to the next stool. He was a heavy-set, middle-aged man, dressed as the man in the store had been—in dark cloth bifurcated leg-coverings and a dark, long-sleeved upper garment over a light-colored under-garment, with a gaudy ribbon around his neck.

"Okay, okay," said the man in white placatingly, and set down before Mikel something on a plate and something else in a cup, both

115

hot. Mikel began sampling them gingerly with the unaccustomed implements. The restaurant man took the money, put it in a box that rang a bell, and laid down some small metal objects in its place. Then he disappeared through a door behind the counter.

Mikel's neighbor waited until he had gone. Then in a low voice he said:

"Finish the food, Citizen Skot. Then we'll talk."

Mikel looked up, frozen. The stranger shot his left wrist out from the sleeve. Sealed to it was a timeporter.

"From TTT executive, Citizen," he said briskly. "I didn't think I'd find you quite so soon, but I knew it wouldn't be long, since you didn't wait to get proper equipment for your journey. It is fort for you that this is perhaps the only place in this era where you would not have been taken up at sight for wandering around in unusual clothing."

"How—how did you know what period—"

"We only had to check the tickets, to see which was missing. Have you the knife?"

Mikel brought it out dumbly and laid it on the counter. The man put it in a pouch sewed into his lower garment.

"I didn't do it! I didn't!" Mikel cried despairingly. He had lost his appetite completely.

"Sh! We don't want a fuss here. I am rechecking your timeporter, Citizen Skot. We are going back immediately."

"I—I didn't even know the girl!" Mikel pleaded, remembering Beti French's instructions.

"We shall see as to that, when we get home," said the TTT executive grimly.

Then suddenly he burst out laughing. He laughed until he had to take a small piece of white material from his upper garment and wipe his eyes.

"I meant to give you a good scare, to put some sense into you," he gasped finally. "But I can't keep it up. Citizen Skot, you are a fool."

"I know that, Citizen," said Mikel humbly.

"The psychologists really conditioned you a bit too well. I am told that you live for your work and have no recreation at all. You are as ignorant of the world as a small child. Come, did you ever hear of a murder in our time, anywhere, in all your life?"

"No. But I know such things occur."

"In the past, not in our time. How could there be a murder in our era? In the old times, people killed one another for jealousy, for revenge, for greed. Such incentives do not exist in the 29th century. The only other possibility would be insanity, and the psychologists would never allow that to proceed to such a point—the diseased person would be euthanized at the very first symptoms."

"But the girl was killed, right before my eyes."

"My poor man, you were a victim of your own ridiculously retired existence. Anyone else would have guessed at once. It was planned that way so as to get a good effect of a crowd in confusion—most of them were extras. Of course all the arrangements had been made with us beforehand, and the concealed telcams were focused away from any Time Travel signs."

"Telecams?"

"World Theater was making a historical crime tridimens in modern dress, Citizen Skot. The girl was an actress. The blood was faked. They thought it would be more effective not to put an actor behind the ticket-window, but to use a real ticket-seller without warning him, just as part of the crowd wasn't warned. It worked beautifully—they tell me your fright and horror showed up wonderfully well.

"They picked your window because they said they liked your looks—I can't imagine why. That was their big mistake. Any other of our ticket-sellers would have waited to see what happened next. You, you dumble, fell into a panic and ran away. And I've had to leave my desk in the middle of a busy aftern to go and fetch you. We couldn't let you wander around here for a week without means of subsistence, and thinking you were suspected of murder!"

"I suppose I'll be demoted now," Mikel said gloomily.

"That wouldn't be fair. This wasn't one of the known responsibilities of your position. No, but I imagine you'll come in for a lot of whiffing, to use a slang expression."

"Kidding—that's what they call it here, I think. Well, I'm used to that."

"And Dafne Dart says she's wild to meet you."

"Dafne Dart? Who's she?" Mikel looked alarmed again.

"Your performance made a tremend impression on her. She told me to tell you she thinks 'you're purely vlumpish.' She's the actress who played the murder victim."

"That red-haired girl with the green eyes with flecks of amber in them?" asked Mikel eagerly. "With the streely smile and the gorge voice?"

"You seem to have noticed her," said the TTT executive dryly. "Yes, that's the one. I thought you didn't go for women."

"But that's different!" Mikel Skot caroled. "Redheads with green eyes—that's the one kind that crashes me and that I crash—I just found it out today.

"Come on, Citizen, what are we waiting for? Let's go!"

Transfer Point

Anthony Boucher

Originally published in *Galaxy Science Fiction*, November
1950

*T*here were three of them in the retreat, three out of all mankind safe from the deadly yellow bands.

The great Kirth-Labbery himself had constructed the retreat and its extraordinary air-conditioning—not because his scientific genius had foreseen the coming of the poisonous element, agnoton, and the end of the human race, but because he itched.

And here Vyrko sat, methodically recording the destruction of mankind, once in a straight factual record, for the instruction of future readers ("if any," he added wryly to himself), and again as a canto in that epic poem of Man which he never expected to complete, but for which he lived.

Lavra's long golden hair fell over his shoulders. It was odd that its scent distracted him when he was at work on the factual record, yet seemed to wing the lines of the epic.

"But why bother?" she asked. Her speech might have been clearer if her tongue had not been more preoccupied with the savor of the apple than with the articulation of words. But Vyrko understood readily: the remark was as familiar an opening as P-K4 in chess.

"It's my duty," Vyrko explained patiently. "I haven't your father's scientific knowledge and perception. Your father's? I haven't the knowledge of his humblest lab assistant. But I can put words together so that they make sense and sometimes more than sense, and I have to do this."

From Lavra's plump red lips an apple pip fell into the works of the electronic typewriter. Vyrko fished it out automatically; this too was part of the gambit, with the possible variants of grape seed, orange peel....

"But why," Lavra demanded petulantly, "won't Father let us leave here? A girl might as well be in a ... a ..."

"Convent?" Vyrko suggested. He was a good amateur paleolinguist. "There is an analogy—even despite my presence. Convents were supposed to shelter girls from the Perils of The World. Now the whole world is one great Peril ... outside of this retreat."

"Go on," Lavra urged. She had long ago learned, Vyrko suspected, that he was a faintly over-serious young man with no small talk, and that she could enjoy his full attention only by asking to have something explained, even if for the nth time.

He smiled and thought of the girls he used to talk with, not at, and of how little breath they had for talking now in the world where no one drew an unobstructed breath.

∞

IT HAD BEGUN with the accidental discovery in a routine laboratory analysis of a new element in the air, an inert gas which the great paleolinguist Larkish had named agnoton, the Unknown Thing, after the pattern of the similar nicknames given to others: neon, the New Thing; xenon, the Strange Thing.

It had continued (the explanation ran off so automatically that his mind was free to range from the next line of the epic to the interesting question of whether the presence of ear lobes would damage the symmetry of Lavra's perfect face) it had continued with the itching and sneezing, the coughing and wheezing, with the increase of the percentage of agnoton in the atmosphere, promptly passing any other inert gas, even argon, and soon rivaling oxygen itself.

And it had culminated (no, the lines were cleaner without lobes), on that day when only the three of them were here in this retreat, with the discovery that the human race was allergic to agnoton.

Allergies had been conquered for a decade of generations. Their cure, even their palliation, had been forgotten. And mankind coughed and sneezed and itched … and died. For while the allergies of the ancient past produced only agonies to make the patient long for death, agnoton brought on racking and incessant spasms of coughing and sneezing which no heart could long withstand.

"So if you leave this shelter, my dear," Vyrko concluded, "you too will fight for every breath and twist your body in torment until your heart decides that it is all just too much trouble. Here we are safe, because your father's eczema was the only known case of allergy in centuries—and was traced to the inert gases. Here is the only air-conditioning in the world that excludes the inert gases—and with them agnoton. And here—"

Lavra leaned forward, a smile and a red fleck of apple skin on her lips, the apples of her breasts touching Vyrko's shoulders. This too was part of the gambit.

Usually it was merely declined. Tyrsa stood between them. Tyrsa, who sang well and talked better; whose plain face and beautiful throat were alike racked by agnoton.... This time the gambit was interrupted.

Kirth-Labbery himself had come in unnoticed. His old voice was thin with weariness, sharp with impatience. "And here we are, safe in perpetuity, with our air-conditioning, our energy plant, our hydroponics! Safe in perpetual siege, besieged by an inert gas!"

Vyrko grinned. "Undignified, isn't it?"

Kirth-Labbery managed to laugh at himself. "Damn your secretarial hide, Vyrko. I love you like a son, but if I had one man who knew a meson from a metazoon to help me in the laboratory...."

"You'll find something, Father," Lavra said vaguely.

Her father regarded her with an odd seriousness. "Lavra," he said, "your beauty is the greatest thing that I have wrought—with a certain assistance, I'll grant, from the genes so obviously carried by your mother. That beauty alone still has meaning. The sight of you would bring a momentary happiness even to a man choking in his last spasms, while our great web of civilization...."

He absently left the sentence unfinished and switched on the video screen. He had to try a dozen channels before he found one that was still casting. When every erg of a man's energy goes to drawing his next breath, he cannot tend his machine.

At last Kirth-Labbery picked up a Nyork newscast. The announcer was sneezing badly ("The older literature," Vyrko observed, "found sneezing comic...."), but still contriving to speak, and somewhere a group of technicians must have had partial control of themselves.

"Four hundred and seventy-two planes have crashed," the announcer said, "in the past forty-eight hours. Civil authorities have forbidden further plane travel indefinitely because of the danger of spasms at the controls, and it is rumored that all vehicular transport whatsoever is to come under the same ban. No Rocklipper has arrived from Lunn for over a week, and it is thirty-six hours since we have made contact with the Lunn telestation. Yurp has been silent for over two days, and Asia a week.

"'The most serious threat of this epidemic,' the head of the Academy has said in an authorized statement, 'is the complete disruption of the systems of communication upon which world civilization is based. When man becomes physically incapable of governing his machines....'"

∞

IT WAS THEN that they saw the first of the yellow bands.

It was just that: a band of bright yellow some thirty centimeters wide, about five meters long, and so thin as to seem insubstantial, a mere stripe of color. It came underneath the backdrop behind the announcer. It streaked about the casting room with questing sinuosity. No features, no appendages relieved its yellow blankness.

Then with a deft whipping motion it wrapped itself around the announcer. It held him only an instant. His hideously shriveled body plunged toward the camera as the screen went dead.

That was the start of the horror.

Vyrko, naturally, had no idea of the origin of the yellow bands. Even Kirth-Labbery could offer no more than conjectures. From another planet, another system, another galaxy, another universe....

It did not matter. Precise knowledge had now lost its importance. Kirth-Labbery was almost as indifferent to the problem as was Lavra; he speculated on it out of sheer habit. What signified was that the yellow bands were alien, and that they were rapidly and precisely completing the destruction of mankind begun by the agnoton.

"Their arrival immediately after the epidemic," Kirth-Labbery concluded, "cannot be coincidence. You will observe that they function freely in an agnoton-laden atmosphere."

"It would be interesting," Vyrko commented, "to visualize a band sneezing...."

"It's possible," the scientist corrected, "that the agnoton was a poison-gas barrage laid down to soften Earth for their coming; but is it likely that they could know that a gas harmless to them would be lethal to other life? It's more probable that they learned from spectroscopic analysis that the atmosphere of Earth lacked an element essential to them, which they supplied before invading."

Vyrko considered the problem while Lavra sliced a peach with delicate grace. She was unable to resist licking the juice from her fingers.

"Then if the agnoton," he ventured, "is something that they imported, is it possible that their supply might run short?"

Kirth-Labbery fiddled with the dials under the screen. It was still possible to pick up occasional glimpses from remote sectors, though by now the heart sickened in advance at the knowledge of the inevitable end of the cast.

"It is possible, Vyrko. It is the only hope. The three of us here, where the agnoton and the yellow bands are alike helpless to enter, may continue our self-sufficient existence long enough to outlast the invaders. Perhaps somewhere on Earth there are other such nuclei, but I doubt it. We are the whole of the future ... and I am old."

Vyrko frowned. He resented the terrible weight of a burden that he did not want but could not reject. He felt himself at once, oppressed and ennobled. Lavra went on eating her peach.

The video screen sprang into light. A young man with the tense, lined face of premature age spoke hastily, urgently. "To all of you, if there are any of you.... I have heard no answer for two days now.... It is chance that I am here. But *watch*, all of you! I have found how the yellow bands came here. I am going to turn the camera on it now ... *watch!*"

The field of vision panned to something that was for a moment totally incomprehensible. "This is their ship," the old young man gasped. It was a set of bars of a metal almost exactly the color of the bands themselves, and it appeared in the first instant like a three-dimensional projection of a tesseract. Then as they looked at it, their eyes seemed to follow strange new angles. Possibilities of vision opened up beyond their capacities. For a moment they seemed to see what the human eye was not framed to grasp.

"They come," the voice panted on, "from ..."

The voice and the screen went dead. Vyrko covered his eyes with his hands. Darkness was infinite relief. A minute passed before he felt that he could endure once more even the normal exercise of the optic nerve. He opened his eyes sharply at a little scream from Lavra.

He opened them to see how still Kirth-Labbery sat. The human heart, too, is framed to endure only so much; and, as the scientist had said, he was old.

∞

IT WAS THREE DAYS after Kirth-Labbery's death before Vyrko had brought his prose-and-verse record up to date. Nothing more had appeared on the video, even after the most patient hours of knob-twirling. Now Vyrko leaned back from the keyboard and contemplated his completed record—and then sat forward with abrupt shock at the thought of that word completed.

There was nothing more to write.

The situation was not novel in literature. He had read many treatments, and even written a rather successful satire on the theme himself. But here was the truth itself.

He was that most imagination-stirring of all figures, The Last Man on Earth. And he found it a boring situation.

Kirth-Labbery, had he lived, would have devoted his energies in the laboratory to an effort, even conceivably a successful one, to destroy the invaders. Vyrko knew his own limitations too well to attempt that.

Vrist, his gay wild twin, who had been in Lunn on yet another of his fantastic ventures when the agnoton struck—Vrist would have dreamed up some gallant feat of physical prowess to make the invaders pay dearly for his life. Vyrko found it difficult to cast himself in so swash-buckling a role.

He had never envied Vrist till now. *Be jealous of the dead; only the living are alone.* Vyrko smiled as he recalled the line from one of his early poems. It had been only the expression of a pose when he wrote it, a mood for a song that Tyrsa would sing well....

It was in this mood that he found (the ancient word had no modern counterpart) the *pulps.*

He knew their history: how some eccentric of two thousand years ago (the name was variously rendered as Trees or Tiller) had buried them in a hermetic capsule to check against the future; how Tarabal had dug them up some fifty years ago; how Kirth-Labbery had spent almost the entire Hartl Prize for them because, as he used to assert, their incredible mixture of exact prophecy and arrant nonsense offered the perfect proof of the greatness and helplessness of human ingenuity.

But Vyrko had never read them before. They would at least be a novelty to deaden the boredom of his classically dramatic situation. He passed a more than pleasant hour with Galaxy and Surprising and the rest, needing the dictionary but rarely. He was particularly impressed by one story detailing, with the most precise minutiae, the politics of the American Religious Wars—a subject on which he himself had based a not unsuccessful novel. By one Norbert Holt, he observed. Extraordinary how exact a forecast ... and yet extraordinary too how many of the stories dealt with space- and time-travel, which the race had never yet attained and now never would....

And inevitably there was a story, a neat and witty one by an author named Knight, about the Last Man on Earth. He read it and smiled, first at the story and then at his own stupidity.

∞

HE FOUND LAVRA in the laboratory, of all unexpected places.

She was staring fixedly at one corner, where the light did not strike clearly.

"What's so fascinating?" Vyrko asked.

Lavra turned suddenly. Her hair and her flesh rippled with the perfect grace of the movement. "I was thinking...."

Vyrko's half-formed intent toward her permitted no comment on that improbable statement.

"The day before Father ... died, I was in here with him and I asked if there was any hope of our escaping ever. Only this time he answered me. He said yes, there was a way out, but he was afraid of it. It was an idea he'd worked on but never tried. And we'd be wiser not to try it, he said."

"I don't believe in arguing with your father—even post mortem."

"But I can't help wondering.... And when he said it, he looked over at that corner."

Vyrko went to that corner and drew back a curtain. There was a chair of metal rods, and a crude control panel, though it was hard to see what it was intended to control. He dropped the curtain.

For a moment he stood watching Lavra. She was a fool, but she was exceedingly lovely. And the child of Kirth-Labbery could hardly carry only a fool's genes.

Several generations could grow up in this retreat before the inevitable failure of the most permanent mechanical installations made it uninhabitable. By that time Earth would be free of agnoton and yellow bands, or they would be so firmly established that there was no hope. The third generation would go forth into the world, to perish or ...

He walked over to Lavra and laid a gentle hand on her golden hair.

∞

VYRKO NEVER UNDERSTOOD whether Lavra had been bored before that time. A life of undemanding inaction with plenty of food may well have sufficed her. Certainly she was not bored now.

At first she was merely passive; Vyrko had always suspected that she had meant the gambit to be declined. Then as her interest mounted and Vyrko began to compliment himself on his ability as an instructor, they became certain of their success; and from that point on she was rapt with the fascination of the changes in herself.

But even this new development did not totally rid Vyrko of his own ennui. If there were only something he could do, some positive, Vristian, Kirth-Labberian step that he could take! He damned himself for having been an incompetent aesthetic fool, who had taken so for granted the scientific wonders of his age that he had never learned what made them tick, or how greater wonders might be attained.

He slept too much, he ate too much, for a brief period he drank too much—until he found boredom even less attractive with a hangover.

He tried to write, but the terrible uncertainty of any future audience disheartened him.

Sometimes a week would pass without his consciously thinking of agnoton or the yellow bands. Then he would spend a day flogging himself into a state of nervous tension worthy of his uniquely dramatic situation, but he would always relapse. There just wasn't anything to do.

Now even the consolation of Lavra's beauty was vanishing, and she began demanding odd items of food which the hydroponic garden could not supply.

"If you loved me, you'd find a way to make cheese …" or "… grow a new kind of peach … a little like a grape, only different.…"

It was while he was listening to a film wire of Tyrsa's (the last she ever made, in the curious tonalities of that newly rediscovered Mozart opera) and seeing her homely face, made even less lovely by the effort of those effortless-sounding notes, that he became conscious of the operative phrase.

"If you loved me.…"

"Have I ever said I did?" he snapped.

He saw a new and not readily understood expression mar the beauty of Lavra's face. "No," she said in sudden surprise. "No," and her voice fell to flatness, "you haven't.…"

And as her sobs—the first he had ever heard from her—traveled away toward the hydroponic room, he felt a new and not readily understood emotion. He switched off the film wire midway through the pyrotechnic rage of the eighteenth-century queen of darkness.

∞

VYRKO FOUND A CURIOUS REFUGE in the *pulps*. There was a perverse satisfaction in reading the thrilling exploits of other Last Men on Earth. He could feel through them the emotions that he should be feeling directly. And the other stories were fun, too, in varying ways. For instance, that astonishingly accurate account of the delicate maneuvering which averted what threatened to be the first and final Atomic War....

He noticed one oddity: Every absolutely correct story of the "future" bore the same by-line. Occasionally other writers made good guesses, predicted logical trends, foresaw inevitable extrapolations. But only Norbert Holt named names and dated dates with perfect historical accuracy.

It wasn't possible. It was too precise to be plausible. It was far more spectacular than the erratic Nostradamus often discussed in the *pulps*.

But there it was. He had read the Holt stories solidly through in order a half-dozen times, without finding a single flaw, when he discovered the copy of *Surprising Stories* that had slipped behind a shelf and was therefore new to him.

He looked at once at the contents page. Yes, there was a Holt and—he felt a twinge of irrational but poignant sadness—one labeled as posthumous.

> This story, we regret to tell you, is incomplete, and not only because of Norbert Holt's tragic death last month. This is the last in chronological order of Holt's stories of a consistently plotted future; but this fragment was written before his masterpiece, "The Siege of Lunn." Holt himself used to tell me that he could never finish it, that he could not find an ending; and he died still not knowing how "The Last Boredom" came out. But here,

even though in fragment form, is the last published work of the greatest writer about the future, Norbert Holt.

The note was signed with the initials *M. S.*

Vyrko had long sensed a more than professional intimacy between Holt and his editor, Manning Stern; this obituary introduction must have been a bitter task. But his eyes were hurrying on, almost fearfully, to the first words of "The Lost Boredom":

> There were three of them in the retreat, three out of all mankind safe from the deadly yellow bands. The great Kirth-Labbery himself had constructed …

Vyrko blinked and started again. It still read the same. He took firm hold of the magazine, as though the miracle might slip between his fingers, and dashed off with more energy than he had felt in months.

∞

HE FOUND LAVRA in the hydroponic room. "I have just found," he shouted, "the damnedest unbelievable—"

"Darling," said Lavra, "I want some meat."

"Don't be silly. We haven't any meat. Nobody's eaten meat except at ritual dinners for generations."

"Then I want a ritual dinner."

"You can go on wanting. But look at this! Just read those first lines!"

"Vyrko," she pleaded, "I want it."

"Don't be an idiot!"

Her lips pouted and her eyes moistened. "Vyrko dear … What you said when you were listening to that funny music … Don't you love me?"

"No," he barked.

Her eyes overflowed. "You don't love me? Not after…?"

All Vyrko's pent-up boredom and irritation erupted. "You're beautiful, Lavra, or you were a few months ago, but you're an idiot. I am not in the habit of loving idiots."

"But you ..."

"I tried to assure the perpetuation of the race—questionable though the desirability of such a project seems at the moment. It was not an unpleasant task, but I'm damned if it gives you the right in perpetuity to pester me."

She moaned a little as he slammed out of the room. He felt oddly better. Adrenalin is a fine thing for the system. He settled into a chair and resolutely read, his eyes bugging like a cover-monster's with amazed disbelief. When he reached the verbatim account of the quarrel he had just enjoyed, he dropped the magazine.

It sounded so petty in print. Such stupid inane bickering in the face of ... He left the magazine lying there and went back to the hydroponic room.

Lavra was crying—noiselessly this time, which somehow made it worse. One hand had automatically plucked a ripe grape, but she was not eating it. He went up behind her and slipped his hand under her long hair and began stroking the nape of her neck. The soundless sobs diminished gradually. When his fingers moved tenderly behind her ears, she turned to him with parted lips. The grape fell from her hand.

"I'm sorry," he heard himself saying. "It's me that's the idiot. Which, I repeat, I am not in the habit of loving. And you're the mother of my twins and I do love you...." And he realized that the statement was quite possibly, if absurdly, true.

"I don't want anything now," Lavra said when words were again in order. She stretched contentedly, and she was still beautiful even in the ungainly distortion which might preserve a race. "Now what were you trying to tell me?"

He explained. "And this Holt is always right," he ended. "And now he's writing about us!"

"Oh! Oh, then we'll know—"

"We'll know everything. We'll know what the yellow bands are and what becomes of them and what happens to mankind and—"

"—and we'll know," said Lavra, "whether it's a boy or a girl."

Vyrko smiled. "Twins, I told you. It runs in my family—no less than one pair to a generation. And I think that's it—Holt's already planted the fact of my having a twin named Vrist, even though he doesn't come into the action."

"Twins.... That *would* be nice. They wouldn't be lonely until we could ... But get it quick, dear. Read it to me; I can't wait!"

So he read Norbert Holt's story to her—too excited and too oddly affectionate to point out that her long-standing aversion for print persisted even when she herself was a character. He read on past the quarrel. He read a printable version of the past hour. He read about himself reading the story to her.

"Now!" she cried. "We're up to *now*. What happens next?"

Vyrko read:

> The emotional release of anger and love had set Vyrko almost at peace with himself again; but a small restlessness still nibbled at his brain.

> Irrelevantly he remembered Kirth-Labbery's cryptic hint of escape. Escape for the two of them, happy now; for the two of them and for their ... it had to be, according to the odds, their twins.

> He sauntered curiously into the laboratory, Lavra following him. He drew back the curtain and stared at the chair of metal rods. It was hard to see the control board that seemed to control nothing. He sat in the chair for a better look.

> He made puzzled grunting noises. Lavra, her curiosity finally stirred by something inedible, reached over his shoulder and poked at the green button.

"I DON'T LIKE THAT LAST THING he says about me," Lavra objected. "I don't like anything he says about me. I think your Mr. Holt is a very nasty person."

"He says you're beautiful."

"And he says you love me. Or does he? It's all mixed up."

"It is all mixed up ... and I do love you."

The kiss was a short one; Lavra had to say, "And what next?"

"That's all. It ends there."

"Well … Aren't you…?"

Vyrko felt strange. Holt had described his feelings so precisely. He was at peace and still curious, and the thought of Kirth-Labbery's escape method did nibble restlessly at his brain.

He rose and sauntered into the laboratory, Lavra following him. He drew back the curtain and stared at the chair of metal rods. It was hard to see the control board that seemed to control nothing. He sat in the chair for a better look.

He made puzzled grunting noises. Lavra, her curiosity finally stirred by something inedible, reached over his shoulder and poked at the green button.

∞

VYRKO HAD NO TIME for amazement when Lavra and the laboratory vanished. He saw the archaic vehicle bearing down directly upon him and tried to get out of the way as rapidly as possible. But the chair hampered him and before he could get to his feet the vehicle struck. There was a red explosion of pain and then a long blackness.

He later recalled a moment of consciousness at the hospital and a shrill female voice repeating over and over, "But he wasn't there and then all of a sudden he was and I hit him. It was like he came out of nowhere. He wasn't there and all of a sudden …" Then the blackness came back.

All the time of his unconsciousness, all through the semi-conscious nightmares while doctors probed at him and his fever soared, his unconscious mind must have been working on the problem. He knew the complete answer the instant that he saw the paper on his breakfast tray, that first day he was capable of truly seeing anything.

The paper was easy to read for a paleolinguist with special training in *pulps*—easier than the curious concept of breakfast was to assimilate. What mattered was the date. 1948—and the headlines refreshed his knowledge of the Cold War and the impending election. (There was something he should remember about that election....)

He saw it clearly. Kirth-Labbery's genius had at last evolved a time machine. That was the one escape, the escape which the scientist had not yet tested and rather distrusted. And Lavra had poked the green button because Norbert Holt had said she had poked (would poke?) the green button.

How many buttons could a wood poke poke if a wood poke would poke....

"The breakfast didn't seem to agree with him, doctor."

"Maybe it was the paper. Makes me run a temperature every morning, too!"

"Oh, doctor, you do say the funniest things!"

"Nothing funnier than this case. Total amnesia, as best we can judge by his lucid moments. And his clothes don't help us— must've been on his way to a fancy-dress party. Or maybe I should say fancy-undress!"

"Oh, *doctor!*"

"Don't tell me nurses can blush. Never did when I was an intern—and you can't say they didn't get a chance! But this character here ... not a blessed bit of identification on him! Riding some kind of newfangled bike that got smashed up.... Better hold off on the solid food for a bit—stick to intravenous feeding."

∞

He'd had this trouble before at ritual dinners, Vyrko finally recalled. Meat was apt to affect him badly—the trouble was that he had not at first recognized those odd strips of oily solid which accompanied the egg as meat.

The adjustment was gradual and successful, in this as in other matters. At the end of two weeks, he was eating meat easily (and, he confessed, with a faintly obscene non-ritual pleasure) and equally easily chatting with nurses and fellow patients about the events (which he still privately tended to regard as mummified museum pieces) of 1948.

His adjustment, in fact, was soon so successful that it could not continue. The doctor made that clear.

"Got to think about the future, you know. Can't keep you here forever. Nasty unreasonable prejudice against keeping well men in hospitals."

Vyrko allowed the expected laugh to come forth. "But since," he said, gladly accepting the explanation that was so much more credible than the truth, "I haven't any idea who I am, where I live, or what my profession is—"

"Can't remember anything? Don't know if you can take shorthand, for instance? Or play the bull fiddle?"

"Not a thing." Vyrko felt it hardly worth while to point out his one manual accomplishment, the operation of the as-yet-uninvented electronic typewriter.

"Behold," he thought, "the Man of the Future. I've read all the time travel stories. I know what should happen. I teach them everything Kirth-Labbery knew and I'm the greatest man in the world. Only the fictional time travel never happens to a poor dope who took for granted all the science around him, who pushed a button or turned a knob and never gave a damn what happened or why. Here they're just beginning to get two-dimensional black-and-white short-range television. We had (will have?) stereoscopic full-color world-wide video—which I'm about as capable of constructing here as my friend the doctor would be of installing electric light in Ancient Rome. The Mouse of the Future ..."

The doctor had been thinking, too. He said, "Notice you're a great reader. Librarian's been telling me about you—went through the whole damn hospital library like a bookworm with a tapeworm!"

Vyrko laughed dutifully. "I like to read," he admitted.

"Ever try writing?" the doctor asked abruptly, almost in the tone in which he might reluctantly advise a girl that her logical future lay in Port Saïd.

This time Vyrko really laughed. "That does seem to ring a bell, you know.... It might be worth trying. But at that, what do I live on until I get started?"

"Hospital trustees here administer a rehabilitation fund. Might wangle a loan. Won't be much, of course; but I always say a single man's got only one mouth to feed—and if he feeds more, he won't be single long!"

"A little," said Vyrko with a glance at the newspaper headlines, "might go a long way."

∞

IT DID. There was the loan itself, which gave him a bank account on which, in turn, he could acquire other short-term loans—at exorbitant interest. And there was the election.

He had finally reconstructed what he should know about it. There had been a brilliant Wheel-of-If story in one of the much later pulps, on *If* the Republicans had won the 1948 election. Which meant that actually they had lost; and here, in October of 1948, all newspapers, all commentators, and most important, all gamblers, were convinced that they must infallibly win.

On Wednesday, November third, Vyrko repaid his debts and settled down to his writing career, comfortably guaranteed against immediate starvation.

A half-dozen attempts at standard fiction failed wretchedly. A matter of "tone," editors remarked vaguely, on the rare occasions when they did not confine themselves to the even vaguer phrases of printed rejection forms. A little poetry sold—"if you can call that selling," Vyrko thought bitterly, comparing the financial position of the poet here and in his own world.

His failures were beginning to bring back the bitterness and boredom, and his thoughts turned more and more to that future to which he could never know the answer.

Twins. It had to be twins—of opposite sexes, of course. The only hope of the continuance of the race lay in a matter of odds and genetics.

Odds.... He began to think of the election bet, to figure other angles with which he could turn foreknowledge to profit. But his pulp-reading had filled his mind with fears of the paradoxes involved. He had calculated the election bets carefully; they could not affect the outcome of the election, they could not even, in their proportionately small size, affect the odds. But any further step …

Vyrko was, like most conceited men, fond of self-contempt, which he felt he could occasionally afford to indulge in. Possibly his strongest access of self-contempt came when he realized the simplicity of the solution to all his problems.

He could write for the science fiction pulps.

The one thing that he could handle convincingly and skillfully, with the proper "tone," was the future. Possibly start off with a story on the Religious Wars; he'd done all that research on his novel. Then …

It was not until he was about to mail the manuscript that the full pattern of the truth struck him.

Soberly, yet half-grinning, he crossed out KIRTH VYRKO on the first page and wrote NORBERT HOLT.

∞

MANNING STERN REJOICED LOUDLY in this fresh discovery. "This boy's got it! He makes it sound so real that …" The business office was instructed to pay the highest bonus rate (unheard of for a first story) and an intensely cordial letter went to the author outlining immediate needs and offering certain story suggestions.

The editor of *Surprising* was no little surprised at the answer:

> *… I regret to say that all my stories will be based on one consistent scheme of future events and that you must allow me to stick to my own choice of material.…*

"And who the hell," Manning Stern demanded, "is editing this magazine?" and dictated a somewhat peremptory suggestion for a personal interview.

∞

THE FEATURES WERE SMALL and sharp, and the face had a sort of dark aliveness. It was a different beauty from Lavra's, and an infinitely different beauty from the curious standards set by the 1949 films; but it was beauty and it spoke to Norbert Holt.

"You'll forgive a certain surprise, Miss Stern," he ventured. "I've read *Surprising* for so many years and never thought ..."

Manning Stern grinned. "That the editor was also surprising? I'm used to it—your reaction, I mean. I don't think I'll ever be quite used to being a woman ... or a human being, for that matter."

"Isn't it rather unusual? From what I know of the field ..."

"Please God, when I find a man who can write, don't let him go all male-chauvinist on me! I'm a good editor," said she with becoming modesty (and don't you ever forget it!), "and I'm a good scientist. I even worked on the Manhattan Project—until some character discovered that my adopted daughter was a Spanish War orphan. But what we're here to talk about is this consistent-scheme gimmick of yours. It's all right, of course; it's been done before. But where I frankly think you're crazy is in planning to do it exclusively."

Norbert Holt opened his briefcase. "I've brought along an outline that might help convince you...."

An hour later Manning Stern glanced at her watch and announced, "End of office hours! Care to continue this slugfest over a martini or five? I warn you—the more I'm plied, the less pliant I get."

And an hour after that she stated, "We might get some place if we'd stay some place. I mean the subject seems to be getting elusive."

"The hell," Norbert Holt announced recklessly, "with editorial relations. Let's get back to the current state of the opera."

"It was paintings. I was telling you about the show at the—"

"No, I remember now. It was movies. You were trying to explain the Marx Brothers. Unsuccessfully, I may add."

"Un ... suc ... cess ... fully," said Manning Stern ruminatively. "Five martinis and the man can say unsuccessfully successfully. But I try to explain the Marx Brothers yet! Look, Holt. I've got a subversive orphan at home and she's undoubtedly starving. I've got to feed her. You come home and meet her and have potluck, huh?"

"Good. Fine. Always like to try a new dish."

Manning Stern looked at him curiously. "Now was that a gag or not? You're funny, Holt. You know a lot about everything and then all of a sudden you go all Man-from-Mars on the simplest thing. Or do you...? Anyway, let's go feed Raquel."

And five hours later Holt was saying, "I never thought I'd have this reason for being glad I sold a story. Manning, I haven't had so much fun talking to—I almost said 'to a woman.' I haven't had so much fun talking since—"

He had almost said *since the agnoton came.* She seemed not to notice his abrupt halt. She simply said "Bless you, Norb. Maybe you aren't a male-chauvinist. Maybe even you're ... Look, go find a subway or a cab or something. If you stay here another minute, I'm either going to kiss you or admit you're right about your stories—and I don't know which is worse editor-author relations."

∞

MANNING STERN COMMITTED the second breach of relations first. The fan mail on Norbert Holt's debut left her no doubt that Surprising would profit by anything he chose to write about.

She'd never seen such a phenomenally rapid rise in author popularity. Or rather you could hardly say *rise.* Holt hit the top with his first story and stayed there. He socked the fans (Guest of Honor at the Washinvention), the pros (first President of Science Fiction Writers of America), and the general reader (author of the first pulp-bred science fiction book to stay three months on the best seller list).

And never had there been an author who was more pure damned fun to work with. Not that you edited him; you checked his copy for typos and sent it to the printers. (Typos were frequent at first; he said something odd about absurd illogical keyboard arrangement.) But just being with him, talking about this, that and those.... Raquel, just turning sixteen, was quite obviously in love with him—praying that he'd have the decency to stay single till she grew up and "You know, Manningcita, I *am* Spanish; and the Mediterranean girls...."

But there *was* this occasional feeling of *oddness*. Like the potluck and the illogical keyboard and that night at SCWA ...

"I've got a story problem," Norbert Holt announced there. "An idea, and I can't lick it. Maybe if I toss it out to the literary lions ..."

"Story problem?" Manning said, a little more sharply than she'd intended. "I thought everything was outlined for the next ten years."

"This is different. This is a sort of paradox story, and I can't get out of it. It won't end. Something like this: Suppose a man in the remote year X reads a story that tells him how to work a time machine. So he works the time machine and goes back to the year X minus 2000—let's say, for instance, our time. So in 'now' he writes the story that he's going to read two thousand years later, telling himself how to work the time machine because he knows how to work it because he read the story which he wrote because—"

Manning was starting to say "Hold it!" when Matt Duncan interrupted with, "Good old endless-cycle gimmick. Lot of fun to kick around, but Bob Heinlein did it once and for all in "By His Bootstraps." Damnedest tour de force I ever read; there just aren't any switcheroos left."

"Ouroboros," Joe Henderson contributed.

Norbert Holt looked a vain question at him; they knew that one word per evening was Joe's maximum contribution.

Austin Carter picked it up. "Ouroboros, the worm, that circles the universe with its tail in its mouth. The Asgard Serpent, too. And I think there's something in Mayan literature. All symbols of infinity—no beginning, no ending. Always out by the same door where you went in. See that magnificent novel of Eddison's, *The Worm Ouroboros*; the perfect cyclic novel, ending with its recommencement, stopping not because there's a stopping place, but because it's uneconomical to print the whole text over infinitely."

"The Quaker Oats box," said Duncan. "With a Quaker holding a box with a Quaker holding a box with a Quaker holding a ..."

It was standard professional shop-talk. It was a fine evening with the boys. But there was a look of infinitely remote sadness in Norbert Holt's eyes.

That was the evening that Manning violated her first rule of editor-author relationships.

∞

THEY WERE HAVING MARTINIS in the same bar in which Norbert had, so many years ago, successfully said *unsuccessfully.*

"They've been good years," he remarked, apparently to the olive.

There was something wrong with this evening. No bounce. No yumph. "That's a funny tense," Manning confided to her own olive. "Aren't they still good years?"

"I've owed you a serious talk for a long time."

"You don't have to pay the debt. We don't go in much for being serious, do we? Not so dead-earnest-catch-in-the-throat serious."

"Don't we?"

"I've got an awful feeling," Manning admitted, "that you're building up to a proposal, either to me or that olive. And if it's me, I've got an awful feeling I'm going to accept—and Raquel will *never* forgive me."

"You're safe," Norbert said dryly. "That's the serious talk. I want to marry you, darling, and I'm not going to."

"I suppose this is the time you twirl your black mustache and tell me you have a wife and family elsewhere?"

"I hope to God I have!"

"No, it wasn't very funny, was it?" Manning felt very little, aside from wishing she were dead.

"I can't tell you the truth," he went on. "You wouldn't believe it. I've loved two women before; one had talent and a brain, the other had beauty and no brain. I think I loved her. The damnedest curse of Ouroboros is that I'll never quite know. If I could take that tail out of that mouth ..."

"Go on," she encouraged a little wildly. "Talk plot-gimmicks. It's easier on me."

"And she is carrying … will carry … my child—my children, it must be. My twins …"

"Look, Holt. We came in here editor and author—remember back when? Let's go out that way. Don't go on talking. I'm a big girl, but I can't take … everything. It's been fun knowing you and all future manuscripts will be gratefully received."

"I knew I couldn't say it. I shouldn't have tried. But there won't be any future manuscripts. I've written every Holt I've ever read."

"Does that make sense?" Manning aimed the remark at the olive, but it was gone. So was the martini.

"Here's the last." He took it out of his breast-pocket, neatly folded. "The one we talked about at SCWA—the one I couldn't end. Maybe you'll understand. I wanted somehow to make it clear before …"

The tone of his voice projected a sense of doom, and Manning forgot everything else. "Is something going to happen to you? Are you going to—Oh, my dear, *no!* All right, so you, have a wife on every space station in the asteroid belt; but if anything happens to you …"

"I don't know," said Norbert Holt. "I can't remember the exact date of that issue…." He rose abruptly. "I shouldn't have tried a goodbye. See you again, darling—the next time round Ouroboros."

She was still staring at the empty martini glass when she heard the shrill of brakes and the excited up-springing of a crowd outside.

∞

SHE READ THE POSTHUMOUS FRAGMENT late that night, after her eyes had dried sufficiently to make the operation practicable. And through her sorrow her mind fought to help her, making her think, making her be an editor.

She understood a little and disbelieved what she understood. And underneath she prodded herself, "But it isn't a *story*. It's too short, too inconclusive. It'll just disappoint the Holt fans—and that's everybody. Much better if I do a straight obit, take up a full page on it.…"

She fought hard to keep on thinking, not feeling. She had never before experienced so strongly the I-have-been-here-before sensation. She had been faced with this dilemma once before, once on some other time-spiral, as the boys in SCWA would say. And her decision had been....

"It's sentimentality," she protested. "It isn't *editing*. This decision's right. I know it. And if I go and get another of these attacks and start to change my mind ..."

She laid the posthumous Holt fragment on the coals. It caught fire quickly.

∞

THE NEXT MORNING Raquel greeted her with, "Manningcita, who's Norbert Holt?"

Manning had slept so restfully that she was even tolerant of foolish questions at breakfast. "Who?" she asked.

"Norbert Holt. Somehow the name popped into my mind. Is he perhaps one of your writers?"

"Never heard of him."

Raquel frowned. "I was almost sure.... Can you really remember them all? I'm going to check those bound volumes of *Surprising*."

"Any luck with your ... what was it...? Holt?" Manning asked the girl a little later.

"No, Manningcita. I was quite unsuccessful."

... *unsuccessful* ... Now why in Heaven's name, mused Manning Stern, should I be thinking of martinis at breakfast time?

Noon

Henry Kuttner

Writing under the pseudonym Hudson Hastings

Originally published in *Thrilling Wonder Stories*, August 1947

WHEN HE LOOKED UP from the pool, the garden was—different. In the water Weston had seen the reflection of blue sky and sunset clouds, and the shape of a plane going over. The deep buzzing of the engines had suddenly died. It had been sunset; now it was noon—and he was no longer in Versailles.

It had taken months. But the miracle was that it had happened at all. People who search for miracles seldom find them. Yet John Weston, perhaps because he was idle and footloose and wealthy enough to indulge his impulses, had come searching for a phantom, and had found it. Dunne had been right, and the theory of serial time could be right, and the authenticated tales of temporal apparitions in the Versailles garden were more than merely tales.

The first day he had come here he had sensed a shifting and a strangeness, but it had passed quickly. Still, it was enough to anchor him here, strolling through the old paths, not quite believing that he would ever again see that face he had glimpsed momentarily through a shimmer of spray. Time-traveling was nothing you could weigh and balance. It either happened or it didn't.

And now it happened.

Weston stood without moving, looking around. The trees had moved and changed, and not far away were low blue buildings with conical roofs. Underfoot was a thick, soft moss instead of grass. The pool was still at his feet.

After the initial shock of incredulous amazement had passed, he began to walk toward the cone-roofed buildings.

Then the second miracle happened. Three people came out of one of the structures and began to walk toward him. One of them was the girl whose face he had already seen. The others were young men, thin, wearing tunics of shining bronze-green, like the girl's, and a curious vitality seemed to shimmer from them as they walked.

As Weston looked at them, he felt certain that this was another world or a far-distant era in time. They were almost unbelievably slender, but not awkward or angular, nor were their thin, pointed faces sharp. Bronze-green eyes looked at him.

Weston opened his mouth. The impossibility of communication occurred to him. But they were waiting.

"Hello," Weston stuttered almost at random.

The three smiled at him and repeated his greeting. It might have been merely a friendly echo. Weston, slightly stunned, tried again.

"Where am I?" he asked. "What place is this?"

"This is Jekir's," the girl answered.

"Oh. W-what year is this?"

But this time they looked at him, still smiling, but waiting for something. It was very quiet; leaves rustled somewhere.

One of the men turned and walked softly away.

"He has work to do," the girl said. "Have you finished yours for a while? My name is—"

It sounded something like *Serena*.

Weston had not expected this placid acceptance. He began to explain and question, but the girl interrupted him.

"I must get back to my work, too." She turned, and Weston, hesitating, glanced helplessly at the other man.

There was no help there.

Weston went after Serena, feeling baffled. She had gone into one of the buildings. It was an amazing place, Weston found. There were corridors and little irregular rooms and floors like balconies, and all the partitions were translucent, like the walls. Lights came in green, deep blue, and ocean-purple.

The glass globe Serena carried was translucent and glowed with a strange greenish light

When Weston caught up with the girl, he saw that she was carrying a globe of glass. Not until they emerged in the daylight did he see that it was apparently full of smoke, a trickle of it escaping through an opening in the top and drifting back as Serena walked.

She put the sphere down on the moss and began her work, totally ignoring Weston. She made fires spring up—Weston was completely puzzled by the method—and simply sat, and looked at the flames. That seemed to be all there was to it.

Twice Weston spoke to her, but she did not answer. He finally began to explore the buildings. In the end, he was no wiser than when he began, and he had not encountered either of the two men. Whatever he had expected, it wasn't this.

He thought: Why aren't they surprised? Had time-traveling become common or was there another answer?

The noon passed into afternoon and the beginnings of blue evening, while Weston moved like a ghost through that strange, incomprehensible place that was too alien for him to understand. Finally he saw Serena and the men sitting on the moss before one of the buildings. He went out to them, and saw that they were eating. He joined them.

It was the strangest meal Weston had ever had. The earth served him! A little pool opened in the lawn at his feet, exactly like an opening mouth. It was full of something like jelly. Weston, watching the others, scooped up some of the stuff in his palms and tried it. It was palatable enough.

Then, around the pool, a ring of small green plants pushed themselves up, budded without blossoming, and put out round fruits like little balloons which swelled as he watched. Serena plucked one and ate it. Weston closed his mind temporarily to questions and—had dinner!

When they finished, the pool closed, and the tiny plants fell to bright pink dust that sifted into the moss. The three aliens sat back, paying little attention to Weston, and talked.

"The fires were burning well today," Serena said. "It was easy to handle the clay."

"I had a little trouble," one of the young men murmured.

"Will you finish soon?" Weston asked, and they looked at him with odd eagerness.

"I shall. I think I shall," Serena answered. "How far along are you?"

"That isn't my job," Weston found himself saying. "I'm from a different time. This isn't my world at all. I—I—"

He stopped, because they were looking at him with polite

inattention. Then they went on with their talk as though he hadn't spoken.

It grew darker. Time in that world was different. Weston had left Versailles at sunset and stepped into noon. Finally Serena stood up and led the way back into a grove of tall trees. Four branches were hanging low, and at the end of each branch was an enormous folded flower. The flowers opened slowly.

Serena stepped into the soft trough of the nearest and stretched out. The petals folded about her, and the branch rose. The two men also relaxed in similar fantastic hammocks. One flower remained.

Weston hesitated, alone in the gathering darkness. He had not had a single question answered satisfactorily since he came here. He had met only acceptance. Even this world accepted him without an inquiry. There were now *four* flowers—perhaps last night there had been only three.

Serena and the men were invisible in their blossom-hammocks above Weston's head. He drew a long breath and turned away. He went to the pool that was that gateway back to his own time, but something stopped him from making any definite move toward return. This opportunity might never come again. He had what he had wanted. He was in another time-world—but such a world! How could he find out?

IN THE END, HE RETURNED to the fourth flower and lay down. The petals folded around him. There was a sweet, cool scent in his nostrils, a warm rocking—and that was the last thing he remembered. The next day—

The next day the two men tried to kill him.

The flowers opened at dawn, and the four bathed in a pool of glowing water that felt like silk. And another tiny crater opened in the moss to feed them all. Afterwards, ignoring Weston's futile questions, Serena went away to her work. The two men watched Weston follow her, their eyes coldly interested.

By now Weston knew he must leave very soon. If he did not get his questions answered quickly, they would never be answered. So he kept interrupting Serena at her work, asking what it was she did, what this world was like, a thousand other queries that apparently meant nothing at all to her. Sometimes she spoke, but only once did she give Weston any real help. Once she said:

"You must ask The Knowledge about that." And she gave Weston directions.

Perhaps it was merely to get rid of his annoying presence.

At any rate, he followed Serena's instructions, feeling like an ignorant child in a place of inconceivable maturity. Yet The Knowledge sounded very helpful. A library of talking books or pictures, or a radio-atomic brain. Weston began to feel rising excitement as he searched in the building Serena had indicated.

At first he couldn't find it. The room looked ordinary, insofar as any of those rooms of deep, cool light and color could ever seem ordinary. But after a while one of the men brushed past Weston in the doorway and crossed the floor to stand before the far wall.

In the wall an oval of shining light dawned. The man seemed to listen. Then he turned and went softly out by another door. The bright oval faded.

When Weston stepped in front of it, the panel came to life again. It was The Knowledge, all right. And it was the equivalent of a super-library. A machine—yes, a radio-atomic brain, a mechanical colloid that was the culmination of the thinking machines of Weston's own time. It could answer questions. Serena's race had come to need a radio-atomic brain, because they had lost a certain human factor, over the long, long ages.

They had lost intelligence.

They had initiative. So has a plant. So has a flower. And their's was the force that activates unreasoning things. The Knowledge explained that, in answer to Weston's silent questioning.

But it was only a machine—it didn't know all Weston wanted to learn. He found himself looking for some human understanding to go with the more than human wisdom it seemed to have—some friendliness!—behind that shining panel, and of course there was nothing like that at all. A radio-atomic brain, keyed to perform certain functions, but without initiative, to give the humans knowledge as they needed it.

Weston got his answers at last.

After a time he stepped outside to get some fresh air. He felt stifled. He could see Serena and the others working away at their unearthly fires, and overhead was the burning sunlight of mankind's long noon.

Yes, it was noon. It had been noontide for a millennium!

What Weston had expected to find in the future was problematical. But he had not expected this—what The Knowledge had told him. He stood there, sweating and curiously unwilling to move. Around him were tiny rustlings in the moss. He could hear the flames roar up, and twice he heard a very deep sighing, like a giant drawing the first breaths of life.

It was noon. That was the answer. A noon that might have lasted for a million years. Weston tried to comprehend it. But he was used to flux. He found it hard to realize that when you reach perfection, by the definition of that term you can't go up or down.

Serena's race had achieved perfection. It had stopped at mankind's midday. There would never be afternoon or twilight but, Weston thought coldly, in the end, there would be night!

It had happened before, he knew. Ants and bees were found in fossil form a million years old, exactly like ants and bees today. And the ordinary cockroach is a hundred million years old in its form. When it achieved perfection, absolute adaptation to its environment—it stopped. As the human race had stopped, too.

Noon....

WESTON LOOKED FOR SERENA. He still couldn't quite believe that she was—what she was. He saw her working with the two men, and amid the fires a giant figure stood motionless. Weston called to the girl.

Noon!

He knew now the kind of work they did, and why it absorbed them so utterly. He knew that they were creating—life. Creating it endlessly, hopelessly, in unstable forms that flickered out or were destroyed as they sprang flawed from the fires. He knew a little of the myriad experiments they had tried and found useless. And perhaps, in a way, he guessed why they worked, and why they failed.

It was clear to him too, by analogy, what had happened to the human race in the interval between his own time and this. He went looking for Serena presently. He wanted to gaze on her strange, vibrant, otherworldly brightness and try to convince himself that she was—what she was.

For already he was finding something almost hypnotic about the girl. Such brilliance, such dazzling perfection, such incredible sureness in all she did, without a wasted motion or a moment of indecision. Of course that was possible to her—as it is impossible in ordinary humans—because she was what she was. Still, he had to look at her.

He found her working with the two men and among the fires he saw a giant figure stand motionless, looming above them.

"Serena!" he called.

He thought: If I could tell her, make her believe what has happened, perhaps she'll really notice me.

She came forward, wiping the flames from her hands like water. There was a look even brighter than usual on her glowing face.

"We will succeed this time," she said, and Weston went cold. "Now that you've come, a new factor is made available for us. You! We need you. The Knowledge has just told us that if we use your mind-factor, we have a better chance to succeed."

He looked into her eyes and read the emptiness there. Her hand was suddenly on his arm, tightening. And she was strong—terribly strong. The two men had left their fires and the giant figure, and were moving toward Weston.

He tore free and went running across the moss, running as hard as he could toward the time-door by the pool, under the bright, timeless noonday sky.

Then out of the moss a subtle rustling stirred again, and

suddenly Weston felt his feet caught and held. He pitched forward and slid along the ground.

When he sat up, he was looking around at a ring of incredible tiny beings—not human or insect or animal. Brightly tinted little beings that shimmered around their edges with an unreal glimmer. As he looked, two of them seemed to dissolve and vanish upon the air. The others, low down in the moss, stood watching with hard, jewel-bright eyes.

Experiments. The failures ... He closed his mind to the thought. Serena and the two men stood above him, looking down with polite, waiting eagerness—waiting, he thought, to feed him into the flames and remould his flesh into—

Serena smiled and held out her hand.

If he could make her understand! Deep panic chilled him. He must play for time!

It could be done. They were not really intelligent. He knew that now.

He stood up. "Wait," he said. "I'll go with you, but let's make quite sure first. There've been mistakes enough already. Come back with me to The Knowledge, and listen to what it says when I question it."

They came quite willingly. The flock of tiny bright things rolled after them, unreal, shimmering. Weston thought of Eden.

The oval window opened in the wall. Weston asked a question, and in his mind and in the minds of the others an unexpected answer took shape.

"Yes," said The Knowledge, "You have a factor of the mind that could mean success. A factor I have sensed in the Golden Light itself, which is the essence of perfection. But the woman here has more. It is recessive in her brain, but far stronger than the dominant factor in yours."

Weston spoke to gain time.

"The Golden Light? What is that?"

"I am not capable of answering. That is unknown."

Serena had not listened.

"Will we succeed if I use myself as material in the work?" she said tranquilly.

"Serena, you can't do that," Weston said.

SHE DIDN'T HEAR. She turned and went out, the men after her. One of the men looked back briefly at Weston, and the cool deadliness was gone from his eyes. For Weston didn't matter any more. Not to them.

He could tell that the personal danger to him had passed. And now that he could have made his way to the time-door without hindrance, he did not. He had to see what was happening to Serena. So he followed the three.

This time he had a better look at the figure being moulded in the flames. It was a man, a giant, more than eight feet high, beautiful as a god and quivering with half-sentient life. But its eyes were blank.

The three humans were busy around a new fire they had kindled. Weston stood watching. They completed their preparations. Serena steadied herself on one of the men's arms and prepared to step into the fire. Weston found himself lunging forward—in time.

He got her by the shoulders and pulled her back. The men glanced at him calmly, incuriously. The fires seethed up.

"Serena, you can't!" Weston said. "I won't let you!"

She didn't answer. His words meant nothing. He could feel the continuous steady pressure of her body as she leaned toward the fire, ready to enter it the moment he let her go.

One of the men seized his wrist and tried to free her. Weston was glad for an excuse for explosion; he was on surer ground there. He swung around and struck once at the man, very hard, hitting him on the corner of the jaw. The man was lightly built. He went down in a heap and lay there looking at Weston without surprise or anger, but with a clear intent in his eyes.

Weston swung Serena off her feet and started away at a heavy run, carrying her. When he reached the corner of the buildings he paused to look back. The men had returned to the other fire where the giant figure stood, and they were working on that, deftly and fast, wasting no motions. Twice they pointed after Weston.

He put Serena down, keeping hold of her wrist. She didn't resist, though once when his grip slipped she turned instantly and began walking back toward the fires. Weston caught her again and hurried her away toward the time-door that led to Versailles and the Twentieth Century.

He couldn't find it. And, quite soon, around one of the domed buildings the giant came walking, unsteadily, tentatively, his eyes fixed on Serena. He was tremendous. He was unsteady, because he had just been created, Weston knew, but he came on relentlessly.

The enormous hands gripped Serena gently, pulled her free and started to carry her back to the waiting men.

Weston jumped on the giant's back and got a judo hold. Serena fell free, but Weston found he couldn't hurt his opponent. The giant didn't try to fight; he merely strove to escape, and he was tremendously strong. It was even possible to feel, under that satiny, pallid skin, that the muscles weren't normal human tissue; they were tougher, like heart-muscle. The only reason Weston could cope with him at all was that the monster was so new. He hadn't learned to coordinate yet. He had only that single drive, Weston thought—to get Serena. Nothing in the world could turn him from that.

And Serena was walking back toward the fires. It was a nightmare. Weston let go of the giant and ran after her, lifting her in his arms. She lay there lax. There was no use trying to find the time-door now; he simply ran. And the giant came slowly after them.

Weston knew that he had to increase his lead fast, so that he could circle back and hunt for the time-door before the giant learned to coordinate. It was burning noon. Time seemed to be playing queer tricks. He let Serena down after a while, but he kept tight hold of her wrist. She had a sort of homing instinct, though the fires were out of sight by now.

∞

AFTER A FEW HOURS Weston lost his bearings completely. The

world of that time was a park. Nothing changed. The whole world, indeed, seemed to be a highly developed machine for the support of the human race....

When he was hungry, the moss fed Weston. When he was thirsty, pools opened. And in all that desperate flight, with the giant looming sometimes on the horizon and sometimes out of sight beyond it, there was nothing except the undulating mossy hills, and one other thing.

The Golden Light. Weston hadn't understood when he saw it. That happened later, when he was exhausted. Serena was untiring. He tried to talk to her. She answered when he touched the right chord and she had a response to give, but it didn't mean anything. But Weston couldn't put away the thought that if he could only make her understand, force her to comprehend the fantastic motivations behind her life, she might awaken.

∞

THE GIANT WAS GAINING. He wasn't half a mile behind them now. The sun was dropping. It would be dark soon.

There's no twilight here, Weston thought. Only burning daylight, and then the darkness. As it will be for man!

He talked to her.

"Serena. Listen to me. The Knowledge told me—listen! I know you're not—not intelligent; you have a different instinct. But if I could make you realize that—"

They plodded on. He kept glancing at her placid, lovely face.

"Call it tropism, Serena. Tropism that makes plants turn toward light. Or taxis, that guides insects. Insects have a perfect life, in a way. Instinct tells them exactly what to do and they can no more resist doing it than they can help being alive. A stimulus registers, on them, and they act as their taxis commands. Listen!

"That's what's happened to the human race—your race! You haven't any powers of reason. You can respond only to certain stimuli, like automata. Like The Knowledge itself. If I ask you questions you're geared to answer, you'll answer. Ask you anything else, and you won't even hear. Do you hear me now?"

It was growing dark. There was no moon. But far away was a golden glimmer of light on the horizon. Weston turned toward it. He didn't know, in the darkness, how close the giant was. But he could still make speed, for there were no obstacles and the moss was resilient and level. The golden shining brightened as they neared it. But Weston was exhausted. His mind went around in circles. After a time he began to talk to Serena again.

"You're not human. You lost that a million years ago. Absolute perfection—yes, your race achieved that, at the cost of humanity. Now you don't need machines. A long while ago you learned to harness natural dynamics, the force of growing things. And eventually the technique of mastering that power was born in you. You have it, don't you, Serena? I've seen you use it.

"So you didn't need reason. You got yourself a paradise and tailored your very minds to fit. So the answer was stagnation—mindlessness—tropism. Serena, don't you see the race wasn't ready yet for perfection? It still had a job to do. I don't know what. But it must have had. Idleness in paradise must have seemed horrible to your race, or they wouldn't have had to sacrifice intelligence to endure it."

He glanced again at her calm, half-visible profile. No response stirred there.

"You've got to understand. Somebody understood once, a long time ago. The Knowledge told me that. A great scientist. I suppose psychological biogenetics would have been his field. He saw that the race was accepting paradise before it had earned it, and so— well, he knew the race was doomed, but he hoped that the search might go on.

"He set them a job to do. He gave them the job of creating life. That's your tropism—that's your taxis. Your own race is lost and damned, Serena, but you're trying, by instinct now, to create a new race, a race that will carry on where your forefathers lost the way. With natural dynamics, and those life-fires you kindle, trying for a thousand years to create a greater race than your own—driven by the impulse born in you, Serena.

"Ants or bees. Alien. I can't understand you or your race or your world. I have only—intelligence!

"But that's the answer, Serena. I can't let you commit suicide. You'd go back to the fires and walk right into them, like a moth. The tropism would make you do that. Serena, Serena!"

He had been walking in a dream. And suddenly he saw that the Light rose directly before them.

It was a tall flower of cool pale flame, swaying a little. The shower of gold that came to Danae—it was like that. There were ruins embedded in the moss, as though once a temple had risen around the Light. Perhaps it had once been worshipped. It was tall as a man, and it glimmered, and seemed to wait.

Weston was ineffably tired. But he knew that a last struggle still lay before him. Or, rather, behind him, for heavy footsteps came out of the dark, and the resilient ground quivered a little, and out of the blackness strode the newest life-form the last men had created.

Weston pushed Serena behind him. He stood there, waiting, watching the reflections of the Light glimmer on the magnificent pallid body of the giant as he marched forward.

And—marched past!

Ignoring Weston and Serena, the giant moved forward toward the light!

Weston stood gaping. The monster never glanced aside. He was trying to touch the light with big, uncertain hands that seemed to strike an invisible barrier between him and the flame. He kept on trying futilely—ignoring Weston.

Serena slipped free and went calmly away in the dark, following her homing instinct toward the faraway fires. Weston was dizzy with fatigue. He went after her, watching the giant across his shoulder. The Titan was staring at the light, hypnotized, trying in vain to touch it with his hands.

He did not follow.

∞

WESTON NEVER REMEMBERED much about the trip back. He must have slept on his feet, stumbling toward the moss, holding Serena's wrist as she led the way toward the fires that waited for her. They went slowly; her patience was fathomless and somehow terrible.

Late in the morning they reached the blue buildings again. The men looked up from their work briefly, and then bent again over the figure they were moulding. "Almost ready now," Serena murmured. "No time was lost, after all. Soon—soon, perhaps!"

Then nightmare. Weston had to exert constant effort simply to keep his fingers locked around her wrist. He was looking for the time-gate. But his eyes kept closing and sleep washed up exactly like a tide rising, so that twice he snapped awake in time to see Serena walking toward the fires. He caught her scarcely in time.

Perhaps the gateway had moved with the time-flow. Perhaps he had simply forgotten its exact location. He searched and searched, in a dull, grinding interval of aching exhaustion, all through that terrible noontide of a race that would soon move on into its night, searching for its own destruction.

A dreamy sort of horror grew slowly upon him. The men seemed to be working so fast. Their blind tropism, their ancient, inbred instinct drove them. Weston stumbled on around the little pool, dragging Serena—

Then he was in the Versailles garden, by the pool, again, and a plane was droning overhead, and he still gripped Serena's wrist. He had brought her back through time, from noon to morning.

And that was his damnation—and hers.

∞

SOUTH OF SUVA a coral island stands in the empty seas. Once there were natives there, Kanaka boys, but not now. There is a walled garden, and a deserted house; already pandanus grows wild, and the lichen and the swift tropical vines are beginning to devour them both. And there is something else, eternal and alien, that stands on the island untouched by the hurricanes that roar yearly along the trades and loose their fury on the islet.

The skippers of a few trading ships know that John Weston once lived there. They used to bring supplies, food and equipment and the luxuries a wealthy man need not be deprived of, even though he lives in the middle of the South Pacific. But no ships anchor there any more. As for the Kanaka boys, no one pays attention to their drunken stories. And they will not go back. They are afraid.

Weston lived on the island for nearly thirty years.

He was in love with Serena, you see. She was the ultimate perfection of the human race. As man strives for perfection, so in his own way he wanted Serena—to keep her with him always—to bask in that shining, vital glow she radiated.

He couldn't understand her. But he couldn't stay away from her. She had never known grief or indecision or despair. So, after Versailles, after he had found that nothing else was possible, he took her to the Pacific island. He built her a walled garden there. She knew how to make the moss and the trees grow; the power to control natural dynamics was inbred in her race. She kindled her life-fires—and she began to work again.

The man lived on the island, too—watching Serena, worshipping her. Watching her create life and destroy it. Year after year he watched her follow that single taxis. She answered when Weston asked the right questions, but there was never any real contact. The gulf between them was too vast. She was perfection—and all he had was intelligence.

SOMETIMES HE THOUGHT of taking her back to her own world. But he knew he could never do that. The two men would be waiting, and the fires would be waiting, and Serena would be ready to sacrifice herself to create the new race that would supersede mankind....

Nearly thirty years. She did not seem to age. But Weston did. And then, one day, the end came at last.

He unlocked the door of the garden and went in, calling Serena's name. She had always answered before. But this time only silence greeted him.

He went down the winding path, and at its end he saw the flame, burning like an unearthly flower, tall, pale gold, swaying in the uprush of its own fire. It lived and burned and waited. He knew, then, instantly. Serena was still in the garden. But she was beyond answering.

It was success. It was what Serena and her race had been trying, for so long, to achieve. The new race. She, herself, had possessed whatever quality it was that had been required—she had, at last, found the right formula for the new life. She was the life. Or part of it.

Weston stood there, watching. He remembered what he had seen so far away in the future, burning in that wilderness of mossy hills. This, then, was why the giant had forgotten Serena and turned to the Golden Light. The Golden Light was Serena. It was the new race. She had used herself to create the next step beyond mankind. She had brought it into being a million years before she, herself, had been born!

And all through those eons, her people were spending their energies striving to accomplish what Serena had already achieved far in their past!

There had been a barrier guarding the light—in the future. But now? Had it developed yet?

In green twilight the flame burned on. It was new. This was the first night it would illumine—but the mind could not grasp the concept of the countless nights to come through which it would burn. Millions upon millions upon millions of nights and days, while the seas shrank and the tides of time rolled relentlessly over the planet. While mankind found paradise and sank into the long, terribly perfect noontide of the human race.

And after that somehow, sometime, it must waken, for it was the first of its superhuman, alien race. After man it would come. And part of it was Serena.

"Serena!" Weston breathed.

And then he was moving forward, his face bright, his eyes eager, into the alien heart of that living fire.

The garden was empty, except for the tremendous flame. Its shining enigma glowed through the night. No man would ever know the secret of its power or the nature of the alien life that burned in its heart, dormant, sleeping—not yet ready to waken and inherit the earth, to waken from man's eternal, doomed noon into the bright morning of its unimaginable future.

The garden lay silent. No human foot moved through it. Only the golden fire burned like a flower against the darkness.

Now there would be a million years to wait....

The Unseen Blushers

Alfred Bester

Originally published in *Astonishing Stories*, June 1942

WITH ALL KINDS OF PLOTS twisting in my head, I hadn't slept well the night before. For one thing, I'd worked too late on a yarn that wasn't worth it. For another, there'd been a high wind howling through the streets. It made me restless and did a lot more damage than that. When I got up I found it'd blown a lot of paper and junk in the window and most of the story out—only a part of the carbon was left. I wasn't especially sorry. I got dressed and hustled down to the luncheon.

That luncheon's something special. We meet every Tuesday in a second-rate restaurant and gossip and talk story and editors and mostly beef about the mags that won't pay until publication. Some of us, the high-class ones, won't write for them.

Maybe I ought to explain. We're the unromantic writers—what they call pulp writers. We're the boys who fill the pulp magazines with stories at a cent a word. Westerns, mystery, wonder, weird, adventure—you know them.

Not all of us are hacks. A couple have graduated to the movies. A few have broken the slicks and try to forget the lean years. Some get four cents a word and try to feel important to literature. The rest come to the luncheon and either resign themselves to the one cent rate or nurse a secret Pulitzer Prize in their bosoms.

There wasn't much of a turn-out when I got there. Belcher sat at the head of the table as usual, playing the genial host. He specializes in what they call science-fiction. It's fantastic stuff about time machines and the fourth dimension. Belcher talks too much in a Southern drawl.

As I eased into a chair he called, "Ah, the poor man's Orson Welles!" and crinkled his big face into a showy laugh.

I said, "Your dialogue's getting as lousy as your stories!" I don't like to be reminded that I look like a celebrity.

Belcher ignored that. He turned to Black, the chap who agents our stuff, and began complaining.

He said, "Land-sake, Joey, can't you sell that Martian story? I think it's good." Before Joey could answer, Belcher turned to the rest of us and said, "Reminds me of my grand-daddy. He got shot up at Vicksburg before his father could locate him and drag him back home. Granny used to say, 'All my life I've believed in the solid South and the Democratic Party. I believed they were good; and if they aren't, I don't want to know about it.'"

Belcher laughed and shook his head. I gave Joey a frantic S.O.S. When Belcher gets going on the Civil War, no one else gets a word in for solid hours.

Joey didn't move, but he said, "What story?" very incredulously, and then he glanced at me and winked.

"That Martian story," Belcher said. "The one about the colony on Mars and the new race of Earth-Mars men that springs up—I've forgotten the title. They say Fitz-James O'Brien never could remember the titles of his stories either."

Joey said, "You never gave me any such yarn," and this time he really meant it.

Belcher said, "You're crazy."

Down at the other end of the table someone wanted to know who O'Brien wrote for.

I said, "He's dead. He wrote 'The Diamond Lens.'"

"He was the first pulp writer," Belcher said. "Most folks believe Poe invented the short story. Land-sake! Poe never wrote a short story. He wrote mood pieces. O'Brien was the first. He wrote great short stories and great pulp stories."

I said, "If you're looking for the father of the pulp industry, why don't you go back far enough? There was a boy named Greene in the late Sixteenth Century."

"You mean 'Groatsworth of Wit' Greene?"

"The very same. Only forget that piece of junk. It was his last grab at a dollar. Get hold of a catalogue some day and see the quantity of pulp he poured out to make a living. Pamphlets and plays and what not."

Someone said, "Greene a pulp writer?" He sounded shocked.

I said, "Brother, when he turned that stuff out, it was pulp. Passes three hundred years and it turns into literature. You figure it out."

Belcher waved his hand. "I was talking about the invention of the short story," he said. "O'Brien—"

I tried to cut him off. "I thought O'Brien predated Poe."

It was a mistake. Belcher said, "Not at all. O'Brien fought in the Civil War. He was with the Thirty-seventh Georgian Rifles, I believe. A captain. He—"

I nudged Joey so hard he yelped, but he said, "I tell you I never received any such story!"

Then Mallison grunted and sipped his drink. He started to talk and we missed the first few words. It's always that way with Mallison. He's white-haired, incredibly ancient-looking, and he acts half dead. He used to be in the navy so he writes sea stories now. They say he acquired a peculiar disease in the tropics that makes him mumble most of the time. He turns out a damned good yarn.

Finally we figured out Mallison was calling Joey a liar.

"Say, what is this?" Joey said indignantly. "Are you kidding?"

Mallison mumbled something about Joey stealing a story of his that never got paid for and never showed up. Belcher nodded and poured wine from a bottle. He always drinks a cheap kind of stuff with the greatest ostentation. He acts as though it makes you more important if your drink comes out of a bottle instead of from a glass on a tray.

He said, "I'll bet some mag paid two cents for it, Joey, and you're holding out."

Joey snorted. "You better look in your desk, Belcher. You probably forgot to give me the yarn."

Belcher shook his head. "I know I haven't got it. I can't think how I lost it—"

He broke off and glanced up at some people who were threading through the restaurant toward our table. There came a man followed by a couple. The lone man I knew, although I never remember his name. He's a quiet little fellow who smokes what looks like his father's pipe. Joey says he's past forty and still lives with his folks, who treat him like a child.

One of the pair was Jinx MacDougal. He turns out a fantastic quantity of detective fiction. None of his yarns are outstanding; in fact they're all on a consistent pulp level. That happens to be why he sells so much. Editors can always depend on Jinx never to fail them.

Jinx had a stranger with him. He was a tall, slender young man with scanty, tow-colored hair. He wore thick glasses that made his eyes look blurry and he was dressed in a sweater and ridiculously tight little knickers. He smiled shyly, and I could swear his teeth were false, they were so even.

I said, "You've got a helluva nerve, Jinx, if this guy's an editor." And I really meant it. Editors are taboo at the luncheon, it being the only chance we get to knock them in unison.

Jinx said, "Hi, everybody! This here's a white man that'll interest you. Name of Dugan. Found him up in one of the publishing offices trying to locate the pulp slaves. Says he's got a story."

I said, "Pass, friend, and have a drink on us."

Jinx sat and Dugan sat. He smiled again and gazed at us eagerly as though we were the flower of American Letters. Then he studied the table and it looked as though he were itemizing the plates and glasses all the while Jinx was making introductions.

Belcher said, "Another customer for you, Joey. Even if Jinx hadn't given it away, I could have told you he was a writer. Land-sakes! I can smell the manuscript in his back pocket."

Dugan looked embarrassed. He said, "Oh no—Really—I've just got a story idea, so to speak, I—"

He said at lot more but I couldn't understand him. He mumbled something like Mallison, only his speech was very sharp and clipped. It sounded like a phonograph record with every other syllable cut out.

Jinx said, "Dugan comes from your home town, Mallison."

"Whereabouts?" Mallison asked.

"Knights Road."

"Knights Road? You sure?"

Dugan nodded.

Mallison said, "Hell, man, that's impossible. Knights Road starts outside the town and runs through the old quarry."

"Oh—" Dugan looked flustered. "Well, there's a new vention."

"A new what?"

"Vention—" Dugan stopped. Then he said, "A new development. That's a slang word."

Mallison said, "Why, man, I was back home less than a month ago. Wasn't any development then."

Belcher said, "Maybe it's very new."

Dugan didn't say anything more. I hadn't listened much because I was busy watching his fingers. He had one hand partially concealed under the table, but I could see that he was fumbling nervously with an odd contraption that looked like a piece of old clock.

It was a square of metal the size of a match box, and at one end was a coil of wire like a watch-spring. On both faces of the box were tiny buttons, like adding machine keys. Dugan kept jiggling the thing absently, and pressing the buttons. I could hear the syncopated clicks.

I thought, This guy is really soft in the head. He plays with things.

Belcher said, "Sure you're not a writer?"

Dugan shook his head, then glanced at Joey. Joey smiled a little and turned away because he's very shy about ethics and such. He doesn't want people to think he runs around trying to get writers on his string.

Mallison said to Jinx, "Well, what in hell is this story?"

Jinx said, "I don't know. Ask him."

They all looked at Junior G-Man. I wanted to warn him not to spill anything because pulp writers are leeches. They'll suck the blood right out of your brain. You have to copyright your dialogue at the Tuesday luncheons.

Dugan said, "It's—it's about a Time Machine."

We all groaned and I didn't worry about Dugan's ideas any more after that.

Joey said, "Oh God, not that! The market's sick of time stories. You couldn't sell one with Shakespeare's name on it."

Dugan actually looked startled.

"What's the matter?" Belcher asked, showing off his erudition. "You got a manuscript with Shakespeare's name on it? Discover a Shakespeare autograph on a pulp story?" He laughed uproariously as though he'd cracked a joke at my expense.

Dugan said, "N-no—only that's the story. I mean—" He faltered and then said, "I wish you'd let me just tell you this story."

We said, "Sure, go ahead."

"Well," Dugan began, "perhaps it isn't very original at that, but it's what you might call provocative. The scene is the Twenty-third Century—over three hundred years from now. At a great American university, physicists have devised a—a Time Machine. It's a startling invention, of course, just as the invention of electric light was startling; but its operation is based on sane physical laws—"

"Never mind the explanations," Belcher interrupted. "We've all alibied a Time Machine at one time or another. Land-sakes! You don't even have to any more. You just write 'Time Machine' and the readers take the rest for granted."

"When the story begins," Dugan continued, "the machine has been in use for several years. But for the first time it's to be used for literary purposes. This is because back in the first half of the Twentieth Century there lived a great writer. He was so great that modern critics call him the New Shakespeare. He's called that not only for his genius, but because, like the original Shakespeare, almost nothing is known of his life."

Mallison said, "That's impossible."

"Not altogether," I argued. "It's conceivable that wars and unprecedented bombings and fires could destroy records. Why even today there are gaps in the lives of contemporary artists that will never be filled up."

"To hell with that!" Mallison said. "I still say it's impossible."

Dugan gave me a grateful look. He said, "Anyway, that's about what happened. The literature department of the university is going to send one of its research men back through time to gather material on the life of the new Shakespeare. This man is an expert in ancient English. He's shuttled back into the Twentieth Century, equipped with camera and stenographic devices and all that. In the short period at his disposal, he attempts to get hold of his man."

I said, "It's a cute idea. Imagine going back to the old Mermaid Tavern and buying Marlowe a drink."

Mallison said, "It's a helluva dull story."

"I don't know about that," Belcher said. "I did something of the sort a couple of years ago. Got a cent and a half for it, eh Joey? Also a bonus."

Joey said, "Say, Dugan, you're not cribbing Belcher's yarn, are you?"

"Certainly not!" Dugan looked shocked. "Well, the research man had less than a day. There was some trouble locating the new Shakespeare's address, and when he did, it was already late at night. Now here's the first little surprise. The man lived in the Bronx."

We smiled back at him because most of us live in the Bronx. Maybe it was a kind of sour smile, but we appreciated the irony. No Bohemian Greenwich Village, no romantic New England retreat—just unadulterated Bronx.

Dugan said, "He lived in an ordinary apartment house, one like a million others. The research man hadn't time enough for formality, so at three in the morning he learned how to operate the self-service elevator, went up to the apartment, and broke in to snoop around.

"He expected, at least, to find something different—to see in the furniture and decorations and books an outward sign of the new Shakespeare's great talent. But it was just a plain apartment—so plain that it needs no description. When I say that there are a million others like it, I've described it down to the ultimate detail."

"What'd he expect," Joey asked, "genius?"

"Isn't that what we all expect of genius?" Dugan countered. "Certainly the research man was disappointed. He sneaked a look at the sleeping genius—and saw a dull, undistinguished person thrashing ungracefully about on the bed. Nevertheless, he crept about silently, taking motion pictures and—"

"At three AM?"

"Oh well," Dugan said, "cameras of the Twenty-third Century and all that, you know."

"Could be," Jinx said. "Infra-red photography."

The little guy with the pipe bobbed his head as though he'd invented infra-red rays.

"Then," Dugan went on, "he went to the new Shakespeare's desk and gathered all the manuscripts he could find, because in his time there were no surviving manuscripts from his hand. And now—here's the final surprise."

"Don't tell me," Jinx said. "He'd gone to the wrong apartment?"

Belcher said, "No, that's what I used."

"The surprise is," Dugan said, "that the research man is doing this work for his doctorate, and he knows he'll never get his degree because even coming back to the time of the new Shakespeare he can't gather enough material!"

Dugan looked around expectantly, but it'd laid an egg. There was an uncomfortable pause while Mallison mumbled bitterly to himself. Jinx was very unhappy and tried to say complimentary things. I suppose he felt responsible.

Only I wasn't doing much supposing because I had the most peculiar sensation.

I believed Dugan's story.

I WAS THINKING of that manuscript that'd blown out the window and I was trying to remember whether I'd used a paper weight to anchor it down. I was thinking of that gadget with buttons and I was realizing how this mysterious Dugan'd slipped from one tense to another—which is a thing all writers are conscious of and which began to have psychological import for me.

But the most convincing thing of all was how the others were looking at Dugan. Belcher was staring keenly from under his black eyebrows—Belcher, who wrote that sort of stuff and who should have been sophisticated. The little guy with the pipe was absolutely electrified. I knew it couldn't be the story because the story was lousy even for pulp.

Finally Dugan said, "That's all there is. How d'you like it?"

Mallison said, "It stinks!" and probed in his pockets for cigarettes.

"What was this new Shakespeare's name?" Belcher asked slowly.

Dugan said, "I haven't decided yet."

The little guy took the pipe out of his mouth. "What was the name of the story he took?"

Belcher said, "Yes, what was it?"

Dugan shrugged and smiled. "I haven't decided yet. It's not really important, is it?"

I said, "Dugan, when was that manuscript taken?"

I know it was foolish, but I had to ask—and none of the others seemed to think it peculiar. They leaned forward with me and waited for Dugan's answer. He looked at me, still smiling, and as I stared at those blurry eyes behind the vast thick lenses, I began to shake with uncertainty. In all that blur there was a strangeness, a something—Oh, hell!

Suddenly Belcher began to laugh. He laughed so hard he overturned his wine bottle and we all had to scurry out of the wet. When it came time to sit down again, the spell was broken. Anyway, the luncheon was over.

When I got outside, Joey was standing there with Dugan. He was saying, "I'm afraid you haven't got much of a yarn there."

Dugan said, "I suppose so." Only he didn't seem put out. He shook hands with us cheerfully, said he hoped he'd see us again, and turned toward Broadway.

We all waved once, just to be polite, and then lost all interest. We turned on Joey to see if we could get the price of that lunch out of him, and we kidded Jinx about the lousy stories he picked up. Maybe it was because some of us felt a little self-conscious. I know I glanced over my shoulder and felt guilty when I noticed Dugan standing on the corner. He was watching us intently and adjusting his glasses with both hands.

Then I stopped haggling with Joey and turned around because—well, because it occurred to me that cameras of the Twenty-third Century could be so small you couldn't see them at that distance. All that flash and glitter couldn't be coming just from Dugan's glasses. Yes, brother, I turned around while Gray's "Elegy" went thrumming through my head.

It could be Belcher or Jinx or Mallison, or the little guy with the pipe, but I don't think so. I've got a pretty good idea who it is, because something suddenly occurred to me, I turned around to give Dugan a nice full-face and I waved.

Because one of those scraps of paper I thought had been blown in my window was marked very peculiarly in red: *Load Only in Total Darkness. Expires Dec. 18, 2241....*

FREE SCIENCE FICTION EBOOK FROM SPACE COWBOY BOOKS

SPACE COWBOY

Space Cowboy Books
Presents:

Simultaneous Times
Vol. 2.5

Michael Butterworth
J. Jeff Jones
Cora Buhlert
Kim Martin
Robin Rose Graves
Renan Bernardo
Brent A. Harris
RedBlueBlackSilver
Douglas A. Blanc

GET YOURS AT WWW.SPACECOWBOYBOOKS.COM